PASSION & VENOM

New York Times Bestselling author Shanora Williams writing as
S. WILLIAMS

Copyright © 2016 Queen's Press

All rights reserved. This eBook is licensed for your personal enjoyment only. This eBook is copyright material and must not be copied, reproduced, transferred, distributed, leased, licensed or publicly performed or used in any form without prior written permission of the publisher, as allowed under the terms and conditions under which it was purchased or as strictly permitted by applicable copyright law. Any unauthorized distribution, circulation or use of this text may be a direct infringement of the author's rights, and those responsible may be liable in law accordingly.
Thank you for respecting the work of this author.

Published September 2016
Editing by Librum Artis Editorial Services
Book design by Inkstain Interior Book Designing
Cover Art and Design by Hang Le

Trademarks: This book identifies product names and services known to be trademarks, registered trademarks, or service marks of their respective holders. The author acknowledges the trademarked status in this work of fiction. The publication and use of these trademarks is not authorized, associated with, or sponsored by the trademark owners.

PASSION & VENOM

PROLOGUE

"**Who is she?** She's ugly." The boy gripped the sill of the window, looking into the room where the girl with brown pigtails sat. She was sitting on the bench with headphones on, writing in a composition journal.

He could tell she wasn't doing whatever work she was really supposed to be doing. She was making up her own words, smiling during the process. He wondered if she was writing a story or a poem.

"She is not," his mother said, sitting down in the chair behind her. They had just arrived at the private gun range owned by one of the family's closest colleagues. She had a *Lifestyle* magazine on her lap, her dark brown hair pinned up. She sighed. "She's a very lovely girl," his mother continued in Spanish.

"She's not *that* pretty," he argued.

"So why are you staring at her?" his mother mused, smirking as she flipped open her magazine.

The boy thought on the question. He didn't know why he was staring. He supposed he couldn't help himself and he hated that idea, so he jerked his line of sight away and looked at his mother. "She's probably full of herself," he mumbled.

His mother sighed and picked up her magazine, simply ignoring his banter.

He turned halfway and watched the girl carefully for a few minutes. He couldn't figure out how she just sat there in one spot and wrote. He knew she was younger than him. He had the urge to brag about that in her face. Being older always had its perks.

"When is Papa going to be done?" he asked.

"Soon, hijo," his mom murmured.

He released a heavy breath. "I'm bored. Can I go in and help him?"

The sound of gunshots ricocheted off the walls and his mother lowered her magazine to look through the square window. She could see her husband from where she sat—a tall man, middle-aged with a tan fedora and a Brazilian cigar clamped between his teeth.

He was speaking to another man that was much taller. Unlike her husband, this man was slender, with a sharper nose and angled jaw. His hair was turning gray at the temples, his face serious as he adjusted the ear muffs and lifted a gun in the air to aim.

The man shot at one of the posters and hit it right on target. Right through the poster's chest.

The woman sighed as she watched her husband do the same.

"No. You don't need to go in there right now," she answered in her native tongue.

"Mom!" he groaned.

As soon as he started to come her way to beg, the door swung open and the tall man that was standing with his father walked into the lobby. He had pale skin and bright green eyes.

His eyes darted over to the boy and he put on a welcoming smile, shutting the door behind him and lowering his soundproof earmuffs.

"What the hell are you still doing out here? You're supposed to be in there with your Papá and me, practicing your aim." The man looked at his mother but the mother blew a heavy breath and stood.

"Did *he* put you up to this? Because he knows I don't like to tell you no?" An assertive hand went to her hip.

The man smirked. "He may have."

"Lion, don't you think he's too young? He's only sixteen." She looked truly worried, her eyes growing wide and anxious. She knew she couldn't tell Lion no. Well, she could, but she hated to after all he'd done for her and her husband. He'd blessed them in many ways—ways they couldn't repay with money alone.

"Are you kidding? This is the *perfect* age, Valeria. He has to learn early. It's the only way he'll know how to defend himself later. We don't want our kids to be wimps. We want them strong and ready." Lion lightly capped one of her shoulders. "Look, he'll do one round and that's it. He isn't a boy anymore. He's turning into a man, and he has to learn how we do things."

"Right." Her lips pressed, almost defeated. She looked towards her son and watched as he clasped his hands and begged.

"Please, Mom. Pleasseeeee," the boy pleaded. "I *have* to learn. Mr. Lion is right. I'm the one who has to take over one day."

His mother swallowed hard.

"Fine." As soon as she said that, he dashed for the door but Lion caught him by the back collar of his Polo shirt. "But be careful!" she shouted in Spanish.

Reeling him back, Lion locked his arm around the boy's chest and then handed him the soundproof earmuffs. "Rule number one: always cover your fucking ears."

The boy looked up and Lion cocked a stern brow. "Right," the boy laughed and accepted the earmuffs.

"You don't want to go deaf, do you?"

"No, sir."

Lion threw an arm over the boy's shoulder and then turned around with him, nodding once at his mother before walking through the door. Though worried, his mother trusted Lion. Lion was a great man. Brave and smart and helpful. She knew her son was in good hands.

Lion and the boy walked through the door and as Lion picked up another set of earmuffs and spoke to the man behind the counter about making an exception for the kid, the boy looked over at the girl he had been staring at earlier.

She's even uglier up close, he thought to himself. But deep down, he knew he was lying to himself. She was really pretty. Her face was round and still baby-like. Her cheeks were rosy pink, as well as her lips.

Her hair was parted perfectly in the middle and her short legs dangled in front of the bench as she continued writing.

She turned her pencil over and started to erase something on her paper, but then her pencil accidentally slipped out of her hand. She gasped, but the boy came to the rescue, rushing forward to pick up the pencil and handing it to her with haste.

Her eyes shot up and she looked at the boy with a wide grin. "THANK YOU!" she said, way too loudly. She couldn't hear herself. It was already too loud with the guns shooting bullets all over the place and with her headphones on, she couldn't hear a thing.

The boy said nothing. He stared at her—watched how her bright green eyes sparkled and her long, full eyelashes fluttered. He was still perched on his knees in front of her.

Speechless.

Mesmerized.

In awe of her fresh, raw beauty.

She pressed her lips and started writing again as if he weren't even there. When a hand dropped down on the boy's shoulders, he looked back and watched as Lion folded his arms over his chest.

Standing up rapidly, the boy rushed over to Lion and blinked quickly. "Sorry," he whisper-hissed.

"For what?"

"Staring at her."

"My daughter?" Lion mused. He smirked and wrapped a hand around the boy's shoulder, slugging him around and walking towards their station. "She's beautiful, huh?"

"Yes sir."

"She takes after her mother, Mrs. Nicotera. You still want to keep taking those violin lessons, right?"

"Yes, I do, sir. I like playing."

"My wife says you're good—that you've learned fast." When they were inside their gun station, he gripped the boy's shoulders and turned him around so he could get a good look at him. "My daughter is naïve to all of this. I don't want her to know about anything that I do. She sees me as her Daddy right now and I don't want that to change for a long time, you understand?"

"Yes sir," the boy responded rapidly, swallowing hard.

"But you have to change. You are your father's only son. He needs you to learn the way we do things, otherwise you're useless. If you don't learn, we'll have to find someone to fill your place…and that means finding another person to end up marrying my daughter one day too."

The boy's eyebrows dipped, confused now. "I don't get it. You want *me* to marry *her*?"

"Not right now," Lion chuckled. "But yes. We all do. We have to form an alliance. I need you for this. In order to stay on top of our game and to keep things flowing like they're supposed to, you must marry my only girl. If you do that, our names will be powerful. And we will be so damn proud of you. But you have to prove you're ready for that when she's the right age. I haven't told her yet, but I will, and I have to make sure you're a decent man. If I don't think you can live up to the plate, I will be disappointed."

"I won't disappoint you sir, I swear," the boy confirmed, and he meant it.

"I know you won't. I trust you." Lion pulled away and turned him towards the area where the girl was sitting. She was bobbing her head now, her pigtails flapping as she listened to her music.

"She's young, but she's smart. She's strong. She's talented. And she knows that she'll have to do what's right for *our* name to remain respected. Right now, I am promising my daughter to you. That means you have to protect her when you get her. You have to make sure that she's tough and able to handle what we go through on a daily basis. Make sure she *never* goes against you. Make sure she respects you, even if that means having to put her in her place—as your partner, at your side, helping you when you need help. Make her fearless in all the right ways. I know how you all do things in Mexico, but make sure my daughter *never* suffers or comes to a point where she wants to give up. Her place is to be with you. *Always*. Do you understand, Draco?"

"Yes sir," the boy murmured, staring at his future wife. "I understand. I will protect her. I will do whatever I need to do to make sure she never goes against me…even if it means she'll end up hating me before she loves me."

Lion slapped the boy on the back with pride.

This was it.

The job was done.

They both knew it.

And from that day forward, she was *always* going to belong to him, even if she never knew it herself.

PRESENT

WEDDING DAY

It's done.

I am married.

The bells are chiming and the doves I begged Toni for fly past our newlywed heads. Everyone stands on the sidelines, smiling and cheering for us, celebrating our unity. Celebrating us on the Gulf of Mexico. Veracruz, Mexico that is.

Antonio has become my husband, and I, his wife, and I don't think I could be any happier.

Antonio's mom stands to my left with a broad grin and watery eyes. She did this wedding well.

With the lavender and white color scheme and everyone, from the groomsmen to the stunning bride, looking spectacular, I couldn't have asked for a more gorgeous wedding.

I smile at her, but I so badly want to cry when I look into her sad eyes. I know why she's so upset. She wishes things were different for me. She wishes my parents were here to see me off.

Though they can't be, I know they are smiling down at us from heaven. I know they are present—that they wouldn't miss this moment for the world.

Their only daughter being married.

Their beautiful girl, budding into a real woman.

Mom used to tell me that getting married younger than twenty-eight was a risk. I am twenty-six. I'm certain she still wouldn't believe that I was ready, but I would have disagreed with her.

It's not about me being married too young, or being too naïve, or anything of that nature.

Her biggest concern was that I wanted to be married to a man who just so happens to be one of the most ruthless men alive.

The man I've married works in the Italian mafia. He can be crazy and rude and downright nasty, but he is also compassionate and he treats me like nothing short of a queen.

He has the power that I long for in a man. He is strong and smart and exudes confidence.

My sweet, handsome Antonio.

Antonio is my life, and he has been since I was twenty years old. When I first saw him during one of Dad's meetings, I became a victim to his charisma.

He has eyes as blue and clear as exotic water, and thick black hair that is cropped short around the ears and slicked back.

When we met, I noticed he often wore a smirk on his lips, but there was something in his eyes…gentleness only a woman could catch. There was a glint in the depth of those irises when he first saw me. And when he did, his smirk slowly transformed into a full smile.

And it was that smile that instantly hooked me.

Antonio is ten years older than me. Daddy didn't want any of his men messing with his daughter, so we had to be very discreet about our affairs…until the day we got caught by Daddy. And boy, was that bad.

"You alright, baby?" Antonio's thick, Jersey accent pulls me out of my memories, and I look over at him, smiling way too hard.

"Of course I am, babe. I'm great. Never better."

"Good 'cause I can't have my Gia baby being sad or any of that shit on our wedding day. This is your day, baby, and I want you to be happy and nothing less." He leans closer to me, stroking the apple of my cheek.

For all of the things Antonio does with these hands, they are always so soft. I love them on my body—on my skin. His hands have warmth that can't be matched to another man's. I would know the difference, even if I were blind. These hands love to touch me.

I nod quickly, feeling heat rise on my face. "I am happy. I swear."

He leans in and kisses me on the lips. "That's a good girl. That's what I like to hear."

I study my husband. He looks amazing in his tux. Instead of wearing a tie like the groomsmen, he wanted to wear a bowtie. It's lavender, complimenting his tan skin.

"You look fucking amazing by the way, Gia. Fucking stunning, baby." I blush harder, grabbing his hand as his eyes run up and down the length of me.

The dress I'm wearing can't be beat. I feel so amazing wearing it, and when I first saw myself in it, I knew this was the one. His mom and I searched high and low for the perfect gown. Antonio said the price didn't matter, so we went all out.

It is June 28th, a perfect summer day for this beauty. A strapless, beaded gown made with yard after yard of ivory silk. It gathers into a diagonal pleat of tulle on the bodice. The waistband is made of embroidered gold, and swimming around my feet are ivory ruffles that resemble the look of soft, ivory rose petals.

I feel so elegant today—like nothing can touch me. Touch *us*. As I look at my new partner, I feel myself wanting to burst into tears of joy. He is mine now and I know nothing is going to stand between us.

We have so many years ahead of us.

I'm ready for each and every single one.

I finally pull my gaze away and see some of my distant family and Antonio's family waving at us. I know they probably can't see us through the tinted windows, but I wave back anyway.

We decided on a small wedding. No more than fifty guests. I wanted it quiet and simple.

With the way we live, not everyone could be invited. Some we didn't trust.

Others would have killed us right on sight.

"Alright, Kev. Take us to the airport. I'm ready to get this honeymoon started."

Heat fills my belly as I look from Antonio to Kevin. Kevin looks through the rearview mirror at both of us and then nods before putting the ignition in Drive and pulling off.

As he drives away, I look back at my friends and family. Antonio's Mom and Charles, his brother. He is only thirteen. A little shit he is, with a smart mouth to match, but I am going to miss him.

A week seems like such a long time to be away from our loved ones, and I don't know what it is about this moment, but as I watch the distance grow, I feel a sense of dread.

I'm not going to see them for a full week. I've grown close to his mother. She's like a second mom. She took me in as if I were her own.

When I can no longer see the family and friends cheering for us, I look at Antonio.

"You think your mom and Charlie will be okay while we're away?" I ask.

"They'll be fine, Gia." Antonio slides closer and grabs my hands. I glance down at his manicured fingernails before meeting his blue gaze. "My mother is a strong woman and Charlie is one of the toughest kids I know. I've got my men watching her like a hawk. What happened to your father and mine—God rest their souls—will not happen to them. You understand me, baby?"

I nod.

And then I feel guilty again from the mere mention of Daddy.

I should have postponed the wedding. We were already planning it way before Daddy passed away. Antonio didn't want to delay it since the invitations were already sent out.

I wasn't so much on board with the idea, but then I had a long chat with his Mom and she basically told me that life waits for no one. Daddy is a prime example of that.

He was only fifty-four. Smiling. Happy. Living his life in bliss…and then the next thing I know he's gone. Murdered in cold blood by who we think was the Colombian cartel.

"I need to hear you say it, baby?" Antonio murmurs.

"I understand."

"That's my girl." He cradles my face in his hands and kisses me on the center of the forehead. His lips are warm and soft, making me melt inside.

He then pulls away and opens the middle compartment to take out a cigar. After rolling down the window, he lights the end of it and my face scrunches up.

"Do you have to do that here, Toni?"

"What?" He chuckles. "I want a nice cigar before we take that long flight to Bora Bora, baby. You know I can't smoke on the way there."

"Those cigars are going to kill you one day. I hate those things."

"I know you do." He releases a puff of smoke, and most of it drifts out of the window. The remainder runs past my nose and I groan.

"We are married now, Toni. Some things are gonna have to change, you know? Like when we decide we're ready to have babies and stuff. Don't you think smoking should go?"

"I'll quit the cigars…but I'm not sure about the cigarettes."

I roll my eyes and when he reaches across to pinch my right cheek, I fight a laugh. Pinching my cheek and smirking is his thing. He does the whole sparkle-in-the-eye thing, and he'll say, *"Come on, Gia baby. Cheer up for Toni."*

It's how we met. Those were the first few words he said to me. I was upset with Daddy about something and needed to talk to him right away, but he had a meeting and made me wait.

When Toni walked out after the meeting, he saw me sitting in the den and decided to sit right beside me. He pinched my cheek and said those exact words.

I will never forget them. He was so cocky about it, but I loved it.

"You are so full of it," I giggle. I roll my window down and take in the Veracruz air. It's humid and thick outside, but the smell of freshly made tortillas, tortas, and tres leches cake is enough to make me want to stay.

This is a destination wedding for us. We celebrated for two nights, and the wedding was on the third day.

"Toni, you smell that?"

"Hell yeah. Smells fucking amazing." Toni inhales deeply, shutting his eyes for a brief moment. His sharp nose and sculpted lips move in sync, and then he drops his head. "I swear if I lived here I'd be as fat as a pig," he chuckles.

"You?" I laugh with him. "After working my ass off to try and stay fit enough for this damn dress, all I want are carbs. I'd take an entire torta stand with me if I had the choice."

"I bet you would, baby." He runs his eyes up and down my frame again. He hasn't been able to stop staring since I walked down the aisle. "Hey, come here. Give me another one of those sweet kisses."

I blush hard as I lean in, but then Kevin stomps on the brakes, causing me to gasp and slide forward. I hear tires skid and Kevin jerks the wheel to get out of the way of the black SUV in front of us.

He swerves to the right in haste, but what stops us from still driving is the fire hydrant that he crashes right into.

"Shit!" Toni barks. His cigar has fallen, burning the carpet, but it's the least of his worries right now. He looks at me, grabbing my arm, checking me for damage. "You all right, Gia?"

"Yes," I breathe, but my heart is pounding. Kevin looks back at us, and for a second I think he is going to apologize for his lack of attention, but I am completely wrong.

Kevin, Toni's driver of four years, pulls out a handgun and points it directly at my face.

I scream as he cocks an eyebrow, and Toni looks up, only to be faced with the gun now. "Kevin, what the fuck is your problem! Put that fucking gun down or I'll shove it down your fucking throat!"

I hear stomping, guns cocking, as Toni rants on, threatening a man with a gun when he has all of his weapons in the trunk…and that's when I see them.

Three large, bulky men with handguns. They have on black gloves, and all black clothing. Really tan skin and beady black eyes. They are stomping quickly, careless of their surroundings.

The people around are avoiding them like the plague, as if they know these men are trouble and shouldn't be fucked with.

"Toni!" I scream, pointing at the men as Kevin pushes out of the car.

One of the men lifts his gun and points it at us. Toni looks back just in time, grabs me by the back of the neck, and forces my body down as he ducks.

Bullets fly everywhere. Glass shatters and my body crumples even more as Toni looks me right in the eyes. His are glossy now. An apology has formed, but I am confused by it. This isn't his fault. He didn't know this would happen...*did he?*

One bullet lands at Toni's ribs and he grunts loudly, clutching his side with one hand.

"Toni," I whimper when the bullets stop. I want to ask him what this may be about, but I can't. The words are lodged in my throat. I'm too afraid to speak.

I tremble, tears streaming down my cheeks.

"Gia...baby, I—" The door behind Toni is snatched open. Before he can finish, he's yanked out by the back of his tuxedo, and a silver gun is pointed at the base of his skull.

I watch in absolute horror as my husband—my beautiful, adoring husband—stares right at me with blue eyes so big and full of remorse.

And with no hesitation at all—as if my husband means nothing to anyone in this world—he is taken right away from me.

In the blink of an eye.

In a flash.

A bullet fires through his left eye, his face blanks, and then his body collapses on the seat.

For a moment, I can't think.

I can't breathe.

All I see is blood. Toni's blood. It has soaked my $34,000 dress. It's on my face, on my hands as I reach for him. It puddles around my feet, but not for long.

His body is snatched right away from me again and dragged off.

"No!" I scream. "No! Stop! Leave him alone!" I'm begging, but I don't even know what for. He's gone. Toni is gone and every part of my brain is in denial about it. "Why are you doing this?!" I shout at the men, watching as one of them drags him off. "STOP!"

Before I know it, they are coming for me too. One of them has a sly grin on his face and it disgusts me. I know he is a pig—they are all pigs—but this particular one has a look in his eye. One that scares the living shit out of me.

It's greedy, thirsty, and reminds me of a vulture—a vile creature that picks at the remains of the dead.

He grabs my ankle, but I put up a fight, kicking him with my bloodstained white heels, screaming for him to let me go. One of the spikes of my heels digs into his tattooed upper arm and he roars from the pain, but that only fuels him.

It angers him.

He grabs me again, this time higher on my leg. He squeezes and it hurts so much that I cry out.

I see people, but they are only watching from the safety of their homes. None of them are calling for help. None of them are trying to save me. None. They are all just as afraid as I am, cowering behind splotchy curtains, or running into buildings to hide.

"Come here, you stupid bitch!" The man clutches my leg, getting a good grip. He drags me across the backseat, but I hang onto the edge of the driver's seat, still fighting—still kicking and screaming for my life.

If I'm dying, I won't go down without a fight.

Fuck that.

I hear something creak behind me and when I look back, I see Kevin opening the door to bend down. He releases a long, deep sigh, and then he leans forward to get closer.

"Kevin!" I scream. "Why are you doing this?! We've been nothing but good to you!"

He shakes his head, looking me over. Before I know it, he's wacked me across the face with the butt of his gun.

Blood fills my aching mouth, running down to my chest. The man that has my legs is still tugging, grunting as he tries to wrench my body out.

But I don't stop fighting. I can't. I don't care if I end up dying because of it. My acrylic fingernails sink into the leather and I hold on even tighter.

"That hit was supposed to be enough to get you to stop fighting, Gia. You've left me with no choice. You're causing a scene now and we can't have that." I look back at Kevin with the taste of hot copper on my tongue.

"I fucking hate you," I spew right before spitting my blood in his face. My words mean nothing to him, nor does the spit. When it lands on his cheek, he acts as if it never even happened.

He doesn't flinch or react. He doesn't do anything at all, except what he planned on doing in the first place.

The butt of his gun comes crashing down on my skull, causing a cracking noise that sounds unreal.

My body crumples down, my arms giving out on me. The man that has my legs finally yanks my weak body out of the car. My head drops down hard on the pavement, causing another splitting crack, but I can't feel it after a while.

All I feel is numbness.

Coldness.

I can't even see the sun. All I see is blackness, and that's when I realize something is now covering my head. Something is blocking my vision.

Before I know it, that darkness becomes all consuming, and I sink deep into the depths of it.

I hear myself breathing hard, so I guess I'm still here.

I hear my heart sluggishly pounding in my chest, so I guess that means I'm still alive.

But I wish I weren't.

I picture Toni's blue eyes when he looked at me with remorse. I remember his blood on my hands. I taste my own blood, and the only thing I wish is that I was already dead.

In only five minutes, I have suffered from my very own decision—loving one of the most dangerous men on the planet.

Loving a murderer.

A liar.

A psycho—that's what they all used to call him, but he was none of those things to me.

He was my husband. He was my rock…but now—because of these men—he is *nothing*.

DAY ONE

The *sound of* water splashes from a distance.

Deep voices hiss and hum. Some are boastful and arrogant. Some are faint.

Pain sweeps across my entire head. The back of it hurts so bad that I wince. I try reaching up to touch it, but I can't. My hands are stuck. I've been restrained.

I snatch my hands forward and backward, feeling something burn my wrists with each one.

Rope.

I open my eyes, greeted with blackness. My breathing picks up, my lungs working double time. The rope around my wrists is so tight it burns and I'm not even moving them anymore.

The sound of water picks up. It seems closer now. My head feels heavy as I lift it, trying to move whatever it is covering my head so I can see something.

I panic.

I rock my body sideways, pushing onto my left arm, giving it all I've got. At first, it's useless, but as I continue swaying, I finally get up.

I pant raggedly, looking down through the small slit, spotting old hay and moldy wood. The deep voices grow louder and then I hear something creak before slamming. A door.

I gasp.

"Check on the bitch! Looks like she's moving." A deep voice shouts this in Spanish. I barely comprehend it at first. My mind is in such a fog. "It's been two days now."

Two days?

By pressing my lips together and moving my head a little more, I get a slight view of my hands. My wrists are bound tight. Almost like shackles are around them, but I was right. It's rope.

My wrists are raw and red. There is fresh blood, and it stings the more I struggle.

Tears burn my eyes, but I don't let them stop me. I don't know where I am, but I pick up my wrists and drop my head, biting into the wide, thick rope. None of the strands come off though.

The heavy footsteps drift down the hallway, getting closer and closer to where I am. I can hear the man breathing. I can smell his stench…or maybe it's my own.

I hear keys jingle and then a throat being cleared.

"Stop," someone says, and I'm surprised it's in English. I gasp, immediately dropping my wrists. I move my head to look around, even though I can't see a damn thing. I see the floor and that's it. "He's close," the person whispers. It's a man's voice. "Pretend you're still unconscious. *Now.*" His last word is a demand, but I don't hesitate.

I drop on my side, and it makes my brain ache, but I shut my eyes and steady my breathing. I try and remember the position I was in when I was asleep, but I can't. The footsteps get closer, my breaths thickening beneath the black hood.

"Fuck," the man snaps. "Bitch is still out cold." The keys jingle some more and then some sort of gate or door screeches on the hinges. The footsteps come closer and then they stop.

One of his feet nudges me in the belly, and I try not to make a noise. I don't

PASSION & VENOM

dare swallow or breathe. The man sighs and after several moments, his footsteps are going in the opposite direction. The gate screeches, something clinks, and then his footsteps continue down the hallway.

I don't exhale until I hear the other door shut.

Thank God.

I push up by my bound hands to sit up as much as possible. I'm wary, though. I now know there is someone else here. Someone *watching* me.

"Who are you?" I ask.

The person doesn't speak, and I think I must be crazy—imagining the voice, that is, until he speaks again.

"Ronaldo."

"Ronaldo? Why are you in here? Are you one of them?"

He scoffs. "You're a fucking idiot."

"What?" I spit, grimacing beneath the hood.

"If I was one of them, do you think I'd be in here?"

"I don't know. You might be a guard or something."

"If I was a guard, I wouldn't have helped you."

I remain silent for a split second. I drop my head and study pieces of my torn wedding gown—the pieces I can see—and my eyes instantly burn when I remember it all.

The blood. The tears. *The horror.*

Fresh tears come streaming down as I touch the silk, my bodice.

A heavy feeling fills my veins and then I remember the most important memory of all. Toni.

His eyes.

"Gia... baby." Those were his very last words.

I sniffle.

"Ah, shit," Ronaldo groans from wherever he sits. "This is why I didn't want them to put a female in here with me. Bunch of fucking crybabies."

"Hey—fuck you!" I snap.

"Ohh...and a feisty one at that. First one I've encountered here."

Confusion floods me. "First one you've encountered? How long have you been here?"

"Six months."

"Six?" I gasp.

"Yep."

"And they haven't tried to kill you or anything?"

"If you could see me, you'd know they've done much worse. Killing is easy. Torture is…well, torture. Plain and simple."

My eyes expand beneath the hood. I wish I could see who this mystery person is.

"Are you tied up?"

"No need," he mumbles.

"What do you mean?"

He doesn't say anything.

"Well, do you think you could take this hood off of me? I can't reach high enough."

"I could…but I won't."

"Why the hell not?"

"I don't want to see you. When I get out of this place I don't want to remember a fucking thing. Though it is nice to talk cordially to someone after so long."

I swallow thickly, but the spit gets stuck in my throat. My mouth is so dry, as well as my throat. I lick my lips. "Is there water?"

"You shouldn't drink it," he says. "You'll have to piss…and there is no pot to piss in here."

"Where have you been going?"

He doesn't respond, and frankly I'm glad. I'm terrified to know the answer, but as I sniff a little harder, I catch the stench of urine.

"God," I groan. "I can't be in here for six months. I didn't even do anything wrong."

"That's what we all think."

"But I didn't. I swear."

"Sometimes it's not about you, but how you are connected to someone they know or need information from. My guess is you are here as bait or some shit."

"Bait?" I shake my head. "No. They murdered my husband right in front of me and my Dad is dead and I—" My throat thickens with a wave of emotion. I drop my head as more tears flow down my cheeks. "This has to be a nightmare," I whisper.

"Fuck, would you stop fucking crying already?"

My head keeps shaking. My body is violently trembling now, and all I can remember are the gunshots. The blood that was shed. The people watching and not helping. And that traitorous fuck, Kevin.

"Shit," Ronaldo groans. "All right, let's make a deal. You stop with the pity party and I'll take your hood off."

"I thought you said you wouldn't," I sniff.

"I wasn't...but I will if it'll shut you up."

I quickly nod my head. I need this thing off. I'm tired of feeling blind. I need to know where I am—figure out how to get out of this place somehow.

"Okay," I whisper.

I hear rustling across from me and then I feel him get closer. He is near my head. I feel him moving the fabric and, slowly, it slides off from behind me. The hood lands on the ground, and he moves away, sitting against the wall.

And it's when I see him that I almost can't believe my eyes.

He's an American man, clearly. His skin is pale and chalky, his eyes nearly sunken into his face, surrounded by dark, painful looking circles. He isn't wearing a shirt and there are scars all over his body.

His hair is dry, brittle, and touches his shoulders. He's so skinny I can see his ribs. Chapped lips, no shoes or anything on but a pair of hand-trimmed khakis.

But that's not what catches me off guard. None of that compares to what really bothers me.

Ronaldo has no arms. They've been butchered—cut from the elbow. All that is left are his upper arms, and this explains why he most likely didn't want to take my hood off.

I don't think it's me he didn't want to see. He didn't want me to see what has been done to him.

I don't know what to say. I'm speechless, and I feel nothing but sympathy for this sad, broken man.

"What have they done to you?" I whisper. I narrow my eyes at him, looking him all over. He avoids my eyes, flaring his nostrils. They've tortured this guy for six months.

"Is your name really Ronaldo?"

"For now it is." He smirks.

I'm surprised to see it.

"Time for you to state who you are." He cocks a brow and moves his nubs behind him, as if to hide them. I realize I'm staring and I feel awful. But I can't help it. The wounds have been sewn together badly, as if they stitched them this way on purpose. They almost look infected.

I swallow hard. "Gianna. But everyone calls me Gia."

"Gianna what?"

"Gianna Ricci." Ricci was Antonio's family name. My maiden name is Nicotera.

"Ricci? I've heard that name floating around here."

I frown. "You have?"

"Yeah. Just last week I heard them saying they were going to crash your wedding. Said they were going to give him what he deserves."

I wince. "Did they say a name of who 'he' is?"

Ronaldo clicks his tongue, thinking about it. "I want to say Tito, Titan…shit, I don't know." His eyes expand. "Oh—wait. Toni. That's what it was. Trigger Toni."

My heart beats heavier. My mouth feels so much dryer. Toni…

I look towards the cup in the corner and scramble towards it. It's full of water, and I wonder why Ronaldo hasn't drunk any of it.

"Is this water bad?" I ask.

"No. But I wouldn't bother."

"Why the hell not? I'm thirsty?"

"They won't let you go to a bathroom."

I frown, but this water is too tempting. I stare down at it, my fingers clutching the foam. My lips push together. They are so chapped, in need of moisture. I bring the cup up to my lips and guzzle it all down.

To hell with these bastards. I'll pee in the cup if I have to.

Ronaldo shakes his head as I let out a wet gasp and place it down. "You should listen."

"I don't care. I'll pee in the cup."

He laughs bitterly, lowering his head. "Well, that's where you're wrong. I had the same mindset, until they came in here, took the cup, and didn't bring me more water for days. Refused to let me go to the bathroom too."

My eyes stretch wide with horror.

"They give you enough to last. Enough to keep you going. Enough to make sure you don't die…in here anyway."

"Do they…do they feed you?"

"Slop, really. But I can't remember the last time I ate. It's been over a week."

"Oh my God." I slink back against the wall, staring down at my stained gown. "I can't believe this is happening to me."

"Believe it."

"I don't deserve this," I whimper.

"Does anyone?"

I twist my wrists, trying to pull at least one of them free. It's impossible. They are so tight. Rope doesn't even seem like the material they've used. This rope feels like chains.

"Do you know who's in charge?" I ask.

His eyes dart up to mine and they hold for several seconds. "He's not here. Won't be for another week, and you should be glad that he isn't. That motherfucker is the one who did this to me." Ronaldo's eyes glisten with pure hatred as he stares at me.

The hatred blinds him, as if the mere thought of the person in charge is enough to kill me over.

I look away. "I'm sorry they did that to you."

Ronaldo breathes evenly, but he says no more.

I should have listened.

Why in the hell didn't I listen?!

I squeeze my thighs together and clench my hands into fists, trying desperately hard to focus on something else—anything else but this. It's utterly useless. The water that is splashing outside isn't helping. I have no idea where it's coming from, but for the past few hours, I've come to know for sure that we are near a beach.

Ronaldo said he saw it one day when they brought him back. He thinks we are in a dungeon that they don't keep too far from the home of whoever is in charge.

Well, whatever this dungeon is about, I hate that it's right next to the ocean. I can smell the salty air over the stench of urine.

Someone came to take the cup, just like Ronaldo said. He wasn't kidding. I've noticed they come in here in regular cycles, every two hours to check on their prisoners. It makes me sick to my stomach to think they are okay with actually having us in here and under these circumstances.

"I'm going to call for them. They can't expect me to just pee on myself. I'm human, for Christ's sake."

"And human means what to them?" Ronaldo asks, rolling his eyes. "It means *nothing* to them. They are sadistic fuckers. You call them in here instead of letting them come themselves and they will first make fun of you, and then make fun *with* you." He studies me with hard eyes. "And I don't think you will like their kind of fun."

Fear settles in. My heart drops a bit.

"I see how they keep looking at you. They'll rip your pussy to shreds, little girl. Don't be stupid."

I narrow my eyes at him. "Do you have to be a jackass about it?"

He shrugs.

I squeeze my thighs again, my foot shaking as if it will help me ignore the urge. I fidget where I sit, staring up at the ceiling. I dig my ragged nails into my palms, hoping it will cause a distraction to my body, but it doesn't. In fact, I think it enhances the urge.

I can't do this. I really have to pee.

"I have to go," I groan. I look at Ronaldo and he points at a corner.

"I'm not peeing in the corner. I can't even use my hands. I'll end up peeing all over myself."

"Then you don't really have to pee." His response is smug. I want to smack that smugness right off of him. I've known this guy for less than twenty-four hours and he has been nothing but sarcastic to me.

Yes, he has been helpful at times, but he is a complete jackass. It's no wonder he's here—or why those men did that to him. He has a smart mouth. I'm sure he doesn't control anything he says.

I push to a stand, scowling at him. My legs feel weak, and my ankles feel as if they are about to break. My feet move across the rickety, cold wood and when I meet up to the gate, I grab it and look down the hallway.

I peer towards the door they've come in and out of. I can hear them laughing. I can smell marijuana and cigar smoke. A TV sounds like it's on, and the slightest thought of home hits me.

I watched movies with Dad all the time and now look where I am.

Alone. Left for dead.

"Hey!" I shout down the hallway. My scratchy voice echoes off the gray walls. The laughter stops and the volume of the TV lowers.

A chair scrapes the floor and then I hear keys jingling. The door shoots open and I gasp as I step back, listening to one of them come closer and closer.

When he reaches the gates, I nearly have a heart attack. It's the bald guy who pulled me out of the car—the one with the axe tattoo on his arm. The tattoo is scarred, and I assume that's courtesy of the stiletto heels of my wedding day shoes.

He sees me and his eyebrows draw together, his jaw locking. "Why the fuck are you standing, bitch?" he asks, his accent strong.

"I have to pee," I say as confidently as possible.

Axe man laughs, looking from me to Ronaldo. "Stupid cunt." He turns away quickly, but I shout after him again.

"Hey!"

I see a few more men look down the hallway after my outburst. Axe man turns and storms for the cell, yanking out his keys.

"You've got to pee, huh?" His Spanish voice is thick. He opens the cell with haste and I take two steps back when he walks in. Axe man grabs my shoulder and forces me down to my knees.

I tremble madly as he unbuckles his belt and whips his cock out. I don't know what he's about to do, but I hope he doesn't force it in my mouth. I swear to God I'll bite it off if it means even the slightest hint of freedom…or an empty bladder.

I shut my eyes.

I can't look.

"Please," I beg. "I—I have to use the bathroom. That's it."

Axe man chuckles. "Shit. So do I." He stands in front of me, his presence overwhelming. Something hot and wet rolls from my forehead and down to my chin. It smells disgusting.

Gasping, I open my eyes and lift my hands to swipe as much of it away as I can. I see yellow droplets falling from the tip of his uncircumcised cock and my belly clenches tight.

The stench of his urine taints my body. It feels like it's seeping into my pores, ruining everything inside me.

My heart squeezes in my chest, and the urge to punch him right in the balls is high, but I can't in time. After he's peed on me, he slaps a hand across my face and then roughly shoves me backwards. I can't save myself with my wrists tied, so I collapse backward and my head hits the cold, hardwood floor.

I groan, but I am too weak to get up or even react. My head was still hurting but now it is pounding.

"Think about that the next time you need to pee." Axe man walks out and shuts the cell door behind him. He locks it up while glaring at me, and when he's done I watch him disappear.

My body shakes as I draw my knees up to my chest. I rest my cheek on the cold wood, throat thickening, body quivering with nostalgia and fear.

My entire body reeks of urine. I can smell it on my lips. My eyes start to leak with unwanted tears. Angry tears. I was so shocked before that I didn't even realize that while he peed on me, I'd already pissed myself.

And knowing that I did makes matters much worse. I reek of it all over. In my nice wedding gown. In the dress I thought was going to change my entire life. Well, let me rephrase that. It did change my life in many ways, but none of them have been for the better.

I look down at my wedding ring through blurry eyes. I'm surprised it's still there—that they didn't steal it away from me. Maybe they didn't see it.

Good. They can't take this from me too. Besides my memories, this is all I have left of Toni.

"That was just a warning," Ronaldo murmurs. "Next time, don't be so stupid." I hear him slide in closer to me. "Look, you want to survive here, you keep your fucking mouth shut and do as they say. You don't fucking speak or call for them. Don't talk unless they tell you to. Are you trying to end up like me?" he hisses.

I avoid his eyes, staring at the gray wall across from me. My body shivers, and the ocean sounds grow louder, almost like the waves are coming closer. I try listening harder, see if there may be some gulls flying around, but I hear nothing.

It's so quiet that it's deafening.

My chest squeezes tight, restricting each breath that I take. Normally, I try to see the positive outcome of things. If I have an issue in life that I don't see a way out of, I remain true to myself and keep my faith.

Well, there is no faith here. There is no mercy or love. I see that now, and I should have known that from the moment they killed Toni right in front of me.

I have to survive this. I don't care if I have to keep fighting. I need to survive...

But right now I have to cry.

Because in this moment, I am frail.

I have been belittled.

I feel lost.

God, I am so fucking scared.

What the hell do I do now?

DAY TWO

"**Do you understand** them?" My voice comes out hoarse as I focus on Ronaldo.

He side-eyes me. "Some of it. Not all." His eyebrows dip. "Do you?"

"I am fluent in Spanish," I murmur. "I understand everything they're saying …but I'll pretend I don't for now."

He's intrigued to hear this. He perks up a little, picking his head up off the wall. "Who taught you?"

"My dad put me in private courses. He used to tell me, 'Gia, we must be smart. We must know everything. We can't second-guess. We have to feed ourselves with knowledge.'" I sigh. "I used to hate the courses he'd set up with a private tutor, especially during the summer, but it took me only one year and a half to learn. I guess it's paid off now."

"Don't share that with them," he insists, shaking his head. "You're better off playing clueless. Make it your secret weapon."

"When we came to Mexico, I thought it would be a great opportunity for me to get to know the culture personally—the people." My chest tightens and I point my gaze down at my dirty feet. "I wish we hadn't gotten married here now. I regret deciding on this place. I just wanted something different—exotic. Fun. Toni guaranteed fun…but he lied. He never told me anything about this."

I feel Ronaldo looking at me, but he says nothing.

"Do you have a lot of family?" I ask.

I hear his stomach growl after I ask. He's hungry, but refuses to eat. If he doesn't he'll die in here and from what I'm seeing he has way too much pride to die in a place this disgusting.

"Family," he scoffs. "You mean traitors?"

"No…I mean family. People you can rely on. People that are probably wondering where you are right now."

He looks at me beneath his eyelashes, his oily hair clinging to his forehead. It's more humid in here.

I can smell myself. I smell horrible. Like I am rotting in my most delicate places.

"Family is worthless," he grumbles. "They've never been there for me. It's probably why I'm in the situation I'm in now. No arms. Losing my dignity day by day. It's what *he* wanted."

"Who?" I whisper.

"The boss."

"Do you not know his name?"

"No. They all just call him the boss or *Jefe*. Never by his real name. He probably considers it a privilege for someone to call him by his given name."

I study my chipped fingernails. "Why are you really here? What did you do?"

He doesn't say anything for a while. I hear the water outside again, the birds cawing. Their songs are getting more and more beautiful by the hour. It gives me hope to know there is still life outside of this rank cell.

"You really want to know?" he finally asks.

And I look up, straightening my back. "Is it bad?"

He smirks. "Let's just say I'm surprised I'm not dead yet."

A door creaks open and then slams shut and I press my back against the wall. I look over towards the cell entrance, listening to the footsteps. They are quick and heavy.

A man with white hair finally appears. He's skinny and tall, but his eyes are dark, beady, and distant. I can tell that, just like Axe man, he's lost his humanity as well. There is no compassion in those eyes. Only darkness.

"Get up," he demands, eyeing me as he walks into the cell. He speaks in English, to my surprise.

"Why?" I mutter.

Grimacing, he bends down and snatches me up by the elbow. My body rocks unsteadily, hitting the nearest wall when he shoves me back. Pain shoots up my spine, but it's not as harsh as the chill I feel when he steps closer to me.

"You're a pretty one, huh?" He speaks in Spanish now, his accent heavy and thick. His breath reeks of beer and peanuts. His teeth are rotten. "I would love to know how that pussy feels. I bet it's nice and wet, right mami?"

He probably thinks I don't understand what he's saying. I try swallowing the bile in my throat, but it's impossible. My mouth is so dry. I can taste the blood on my lips every time I move them. They are chapped beyond repair.

My eyes shoot over his shoulder at Ronaldo. He simply shakes his head, most likely telling me that I should say and do nothing.

"Don't worry that tight little pussy." He grabs my wrists and yanks me forward. The pain from the tug burns deep. I gasp as he clutches my face in hand. "I'll let the boss have the honors before he lets us do what we want with you." Shoving me back against the wall, he pulls out a knife and cuts through the rope. The blade is so close to my skin that I feel it's coolness.

He watches me closely, refusing to look away. As soon as my arms are free, I slide down the wall, relieved.

I bring my hands up to study my bruised wrists. I almost want to cry because I can see whiteness beneath the cuts. I'm surprised I haven't lost feelings in my hands yet.

The man focuses on my face. His beady eyes trace the outline of my cleavage, and then he steps closer with a sneer. "Get comfortable in here. You won't be going anywhere for a while."

I look away, staring at the ground. When he walks to the cell door with the rope, he locks it behind him and then walks off, but not before eyeballing me again. He still has a sly grin on his face, and seeing it makes my skin crawl.

When I hear the door slam, I finally release a breath, sliding my back down the wall as I rub my raw wrists.

Ronaldo looks at my wrists before shifting his eyes up to meet mine. "Better?"

"Much better."

"Don't get too comfortable," he says as he lies on his back and stares up at the ceiling. "They never leave you alone for long. Welcome to hell, Gia."

DAY THREE

I was only twenty-two when Toni told me he loved me. It was random but I will never be able to forget it.

"Gia baby...you know you're my world. My girl. My giiirrrlll!" Toni's voice screeched as he played his acoustic guitar. He sounded terrible with his deep, gravelly voice. I laughed so damn hard, and he dropped his guitar so quick, it seemed unreal. His face turned serious, but his eyes were still playful.

"What?" he asked rhetorically. "You don't like my song, Gia baby?"

"You sound like road kill," I teased.

"But you love this road kill's cock, huh?" He stood up from the recliner in the corner of my bedroom, walked towards my bed where I was sitting, and slid between my legs.

I glanced at the door, giggling as I pushed his chest. "Toni, stop. Daddy is right downstairs."

"So what? I'm tired of fucking hiding this, Gia. You're my fucking woman. I *fucking love you and I shouldn't have to pretend I fucking don't."*

My eyes grew as wide as discs. I studied his face, searching for the bullshit behind his statement. But his face was so damn sincere and his blue eyes were so clear. There was no trace of a lie. No shame. He meant it.

"You love me?" I asked, stroking his cheek.

"With all of my fucking heart, baby. And I'm going to marry the shit out of you one day. You hear me? I mean it. I want you, baby. You." He kissed me on the lips. "Nobody else but you, Gia baby."

"Wake up. Eat." The tip of Axe Man's boot nudges me in the ribs. I roll over weakly, focusing on the slop on the plate.

"What the hell is this?" I hiss. I don't even sound like myself anymore. I sound disgusting.

"Food, bitch. Now eat."

I glance at Ronaldo. He shakes his head and I take that as a sign not to argue right now. Instead of doing what I feel deep in my soul—which is grabbing a handful of the pig slop, tossing it in Axe Man's face, and then kicking him in the balls before making a run for it—I sit up and study it.

It's brown and pink in some places. Corn sticks out of it, as well as some other shit I don't want to know the name of. On the side is a slice of dry sandwich bread and a half rotten apple.

Axe Man walks back to the cell door and stomps away.

I watch him until he's disappeared. I hear the door creak on its hinges and then slam shut, echoing through the hallway.

"Hope you'll enjoy drinking your spit after eating that," Ronaldo says.

I press my dry lips together. "Do you want some?"

"Nah, I'm good. You shouldn't eat it either. I know you're hungry but it'll give you a serious case of the shits."

I groan, shoving the tray away. Scooting towards the wall, I rest my back on it and stare up at the window above. It's too high to reach. Even if Ronaldo gave me a boost, I wouldn't be able to get a good look.

I try and imagine the beach. I bet it's lovely—a shimmery, turquoise blue with seagulls and white sand. I hear the gulls often. It's like they talk to me sometimes—

demanding that I find a way out of this shithole.

"I need to get out of here," I murmur.

"You and me both." Ronaldo drops his head, focusing on the loose hay on the floor. "You asked me about my family. Did you have a lot of family and friends where you came from?"

I laugh. "Well, my mom and dad died not too long ago. Mom passed away first. Never had any siblings. I had a ton of friends—but I wouldn't exactly call them *friends*. More like…acquaintances." I clear my throat. "All I really needed was Antonio. He was my best friend. My lover. Protector…for a while anyway."

"Marriage is a fucking joke," he states with snide.

I frown. "No it's not. Marriage is beautiful. It's two spirits coming together and bonding into one."

"All smoke and mirrors. Straight bullshit."

I cross my arms. "I take it you've never been in love."

"Oh, I have." He looks up at the ceiling. "Loved her for eight years. Asked her to marry me, she said she couldn't because I was too unpredictable. What the fuck did she expect after knowing me for eight years. She was a waste of my goddamn time."

"That's only one woman and she clearly didn't love you if she said something like that after you asked for her hand in marriage. There are plenty of other women out there—"

"No, see, I'm going to stop you right there." He lifted one of his stubby arms, scowling at me. "I won't be getting out of this fucking place. Never. So don't sit in here and spew that false hope and bullshit. Plus, even if I did, what bitch would want me now? No fucking arms. Not a damn thing to give. I'm grateful they haven't chopped my fucking cock off yet."

My heart pounds as he stares me right in the eyes. "This isn't a fucking vacation. There is no fucking hope here, don't you get that? You can pretend something good will happen, but I've seen fuckers with the same mindset as you come in and out of this place and never return. I've seen some come back and end up fucking dying right in front of me. I've seen it all, so don't feed me some shit that you don't even fucking believe. We aren't getting out of here intact. The sooner you accept that, the better off you'll be."

His jaw flexes as he presses his back to the wall.

The cell is quiet for a long time. So long that I feel panic settle deep in my bloodstream. I stand up and pace the cell, focusing on the window.

Ronaldo sighs heavily. "What the fuck are you doing?"

"Thinking."

"About what?"

"How to get the hell out of this place."

"Did you not listen to a word I just said? You're not getting out of here unless they want you to! So just sit the fuck down and shut up. Accept it and move on."

"No," I hiss. "I won't accept this! I will not die in this place. I don't care if I have to fight my way out. I will get out of here. I swear it on my dead husband's soul I will."

Ronaldo grunts, snatching his gaze away. He sports an amused grin on his face, his head moving from left to right.

"Did I say something funny?" I snap.

"Not at all. I'm just glad to know you've accepted something."

"What do you mean?"

"I'm glad you've accepted the fact that these fuckers took your husband away…and that you'll never get him back, even if you do get out of this shitty place."

I don't know why, but his words hit me hard. Way too hard. Why did I admit that out loud? I've had dreams that Toni is alive. Some feel so real that it seems all I need to do is escape this place and make my way back to him.

Has it really come to this? Exactly what in the hell am I fighting for? I have no family. My father was brutally murdered and my mother got brain cancer that may as well have eaten her alive.

I have no one.

I have *nothing*.

There's Toni's family—his mom and Charlie, but what use would I be to them? Returning without him?

"Wow," I breathe as I slump down in a corner. I wrap my arms around my knees. "I…I really have nothing to go back to. No one. Is that the reality I face?"

"Your reality is here and you should focus on that for now. You can think about escaping, but you have to be smart if you want to survive. You may lose a few limbs in the process, but at least you'd still be breathing."

"Fuck that," I spit. "I'm not losing anything."

"That's where you're wrong, sweetheart. You've already lost something."

I pick my head up to look at him, my curiosity outweighing my anger. "What?"

"Your innocence. Your peace of mind. You would *kill* just to get out of here, right?"

"Yes, I would." And I am so serious. I will do anything to get out.

"Any person in their right mind wouldn't go as deep as killing, no matter how tough shit gets."

"But those pricks deserve it. Especially the one with the axe tattoo."

"You won't be able to kill him," he confides, "but you can hurt him."

I drop my arms. "What are you saying?"

"I don't know if you've noticed, but he carries a pocket knife in his back pocket. Hardly ever uses it."

"So? They all have weapons."

"Yes, to show authority. He'll notice a gun missing right away, but a pocketknife…I don't think so. Not right away at least. That's why when you get it—and you will—you have to think fast. No hesitation."

"But I thought you said there was no way out of here."

"Oh there's not, but their boss comes home in two days."

"And…?"

"Let's just say causing a scene is the only hope you have."

I look towards the cell door, licking my lips. "Tell me about the boss," I murmur.

"He's ruthless, that's for damn sure. Shows no compassion whatsoever. He's violent as fuck, but there is one thing about him that is his downfall…"

"What?"

"Any man's downfall…"

I frown.

"Pussy," he hisses, rolling his eyes. "You have one. Be smart and fucking use it."

"If you think I'll willingly give my body to any of them, you're just as crazy as them!"

"I didn't say all of them. Just him."

"How in the hell am I supposed to make him want me when I look like this?

I smell like piss and my hair is a matted mess. My nails are chipped and my lips are bleeding."

"Gia," Ronaldo chuckles. "Okay, so maybe I was being a little harsh about finding a way out of here. There is always a way out of something, but with a place like this, it won't come easy."

"So what do you suggest I do?"

He smirks. "You already heard my thoughts. It's simple. Make the king *notice* you…or die trying. Either way, you'll still be out of this place."

DAY FOUR

I *can hear a* woman talking. Her voice isn't light or sweet. It's kind of angry.

My legs are bouncing, the urge to pee way too high.

"I should try right now," I whisper to Ronaldo.

He looks up at me, tossing his greasy hair back. "You should."

Those words are all I need to hear. I push up on my hands until I'm standing up straight. I walk to the cell door, gripping the cold, hard steel. "Hey!" I shout.

The commotion comes to a cease from wherever they are. The door is yanked open in an instant and Axe Man comes storming down the hallway, his hand on the gun he has in the holder.

"When the fuck will you learn, bitch?"

A woman steps up behind him. She has long black hair and a black baseball cap on. Her hair is board straight, her thin eyes focused on me. She looks me up and down. "When the fuck did we get a bitch?" she asks in Spanish.

"Couple days ago. Bitch is starting to piss me off."

"What the hell do you want?" she demands in English.

"I…have to pee."

Axe Man chuckles, and the sound of it is like nails to a chalkboard. Irritating. "You're really doing this shit again? What the fuck did I tell you?"

"You didn't tell me anything," I respond boldly.

He clenches his fist and steps forward, gripping the metal bar. "What the fuck did I just say to me?"

The woman rolls her eyes, planting her hands on her hips. "Just let her go to the fucking bathroom. She doesn't have a cock. We can't just aim and piss in the fucking corner like you slobs can." Axe Man looks back at her with a tilted eyebrow. She shrugs, stepping sideways. "It's filthy in there anyway. No one's cleaned the shit in fucking months. Might as well let her use it. Wipe her piss with that stupid dress."

Axe Man finds delight in her last statement. He sneers, pulling out his keys and unlocking the door. The lock is loud, and the bolt clinks and echoes through the cell. I glance back at Ronaldo.

He's not looking at us.

"Since you have a pussy, you take her." Axe Man grips my arm and shoves me into the woman's chest. She throws me off and I land flat on my ass with a grunt as she grimaces at him.

"Fuck you, you fat fuck!"

He sniggers as he walks past her and makes his way back to the room they came out of. When he shuts the door behind him, she frowns down at me.

"Get your stupid ass up," she snaps. "You have to pee, don't you? Well, go. Before I change my fucking mind."

I stand feebly, turning in the direction she points to and walking.

I spot a door to the right and she pushes it open.

Christ.

She wasn't kidding when she said it's filthy.

This bathroom is disgusting. The walls are covered in shit, grime, and other things I don't want to know the names of. The toilet is stained brown and yellow, with green mold riding along the bottom and running up one of the walls. The sink is molded too, rusty around the knobs.

She shoves me in and I look around, cupping my mouth and nose. It smells horrid in here.

"Go ahead." I turn back and she's smirking. "Pee."

Truth be told, I'd much rather pee on myself again. I gather my dress up as much as I can and squat over the toilet seat. It takes a while for my pee to come out. I'm not sure if it's because I'm afraid I'll catch a disease in this bathroom, because the woman guard is watching me like a hawk, or both.

Finally, after she snaps at me for taking so long, I pee. It's the longest pee of my damn life, and it feels so great to empty my full bladder.

Once I'm finished, I stand and drop my dress. Dribbles run down my thighs. There is no tissue, so I have no choice but to rub the dress between my legs to get rid of them.

I drag my eyes back up to hers and she steps back, her hand on the gun in her holster.

"Thank you," I murmur, walking past her.

"Don't fucking thank me." Her hand presses on the center of my back and she shoves me forward. "Hurry up to the fucking cell."

I meet at the door and she unlocks it. I walk in, side-eyeing her once before dropping down in my corner. She locks it up behind her with her eyes on me, shaking her head slowly before walking off.

When I know she's gone, I sigh. "I couldn't get it," I whisper to Ronaldo.

"Don't worry about it. Maybe tomorrow."

DAY FIVE

"**You have to** make a scene this time. Test your limits." Ronaldo slides closer, looking me hard in the eyes. "It's the only way he'll take you seriously."

"What should I do?"

"Demand something from him. Act like they owe you…"

"Won't they kill me for doing that?"

"If they had the option to kill you, you'd be dead by now. My guess is that the boss has told them to leave you alone until he sees you for himself."

"Why would he do that?"

"Because he has to know what he's dealing with…and probably find out what you know before he makes a final decision. He's crazy, but he's no fool."

"Well, what should I demand?"

"Think of something you want right now. Something to eat that they could easily get but you know they won't."

I drop my head, staring down at the gray floor. "Okay," I whisper. "I think I know."

When the sun is about to set, a door slams shut and footsteps are coming down the hallway. My hands are shaking violently, my pulse accelerating. I'm terrified to do this, but I have to if I want to get out of here.

Axe Man appears with a foam cup in hand, his eyes trained on me. When he walks in, he places the cup down on the middle of the floor and says, "Drink up…or don't. I don't really give a fuck."

I frown at the cup, standing rapidly. "I don't want water! Give me something fruity to drink! Juice or soda. Something!"

He looks at me as if I've lost my damn mind. Perhaps I have. His eyes grow wide, and his shoulders square up.

"What the fuck did you say?" he growls.

"I said give me something fruity to drink. Now." I'm so glad my voice doesn't tremble, but my entire body is shaking.

Axe Man looks around the cell, laughing dryly. Ronaldo hasn't made a move.

Before I know it, Axe Man puts on a deep scowl and then charges my way, gripping me by the hair and slamming my head against the wall.

"What a dumb fucking one you are."

As he holds me, I haul him closer, pretending to put up a fight, but really my hands are on a search. I pinch some of the fat on his side, scratch at his back. He doesn't budge. His hot, smelly breath runs past my nose. It reeks like shit.

When I grunt and pinch his nipple, he brings his other hand up and slaps me with it. The sting is crucial, so crucial that I crumble a bit, my ears ringing. As I fall, I strike him with one hand, the other yanking on his pocket.

"BITCH!" He releases my hair and tosses me on the ground. I collapse on my side, landing roughly on my right arm. I squeeze the prize in my hand though, and take the blows he gives me as he kicks me in the stomach and the chest.

Something feels like it cracks inside me but I'm not even sure where it is. When he reaches down again to snatch me up by the hair, he gets close to my face, seething before whacking me across the cheek with his large, rough hand.

PASSION & VENOM

I groan, feeling a chill cloak my body as he drops my head on the ground again.

I hear a loud *BOOM* and then there are heavy footsteps rushing our way. Several men come rushing in, yanking Axe Man away and tossing him outside the cell.

The white haired man grips him by the front of his shirt, furious. He speaks to him in their native tongue. I can tell he's pissed at him, not proud. I hear the words *Jefe* and *muy furioso* in one sentence and I know what that means.

The boss will be angry with him for what he's done.

"He'll be here soon so calm the fuck down. You know we can't fucking kill her," he hisses in Spanish. "We aren't even supposed to be near her, you fucking dumbass! You better hope she isn't fucking bruised later." He pushes Axe Man forward, down the hallway. "Get the fuck out of here!"

The men follow after him, but the woman is last. She locks the door behind her, giving me a thorough look over before walking off.

I gasp for breath, struggling to sit up. My stomach is sore and my chest hurts like hell, but that pain doesn't amount to the power I feel right now.

I stare at Ronaldo beneath my eyelashes, dangling the pocketknife in front of me.

When he sees it, his smile grows so wide I think his face might break.

"Damn. Didn't think you had it in you."

He's surprised…

He shouldn't be.

This is only the beginning.

DAY SIX

Around dawn, the white haired man comes in with a tray of food. There's something different about the food today. It's not slop. It's not cold or frozen. It doesn't look like it will give you explosive diarrhea.

It looks...*delicious*.

There is enough for two people, and when he places it down on the floor, we inch in closer to see what it is exactly. Toast, a boiled egg, and slices of watermelon. Granted, the toast is dry, but that's okay. I'll still eat it.

"Eat," the man demands. "And don't waste any of it."

He walks out without looking back, locking the door. Ronaldo and I look at each other with confused expressions, well I'm confused more than he is.

"They've stepped up. They only do that when he's returned," Ronaldo murmurs. And then he cocks an eyebrow. "Are you ready?"

I tap my left breast, where I have the pocketknife hidden. "I am."

After we eat the meal that honestly has made me feel like a brand new person,

PASSION & VENOM

I kindly ask Ronaldo to turn away so I can pee. I'm not going back to that damn bathroom. I'd rather pee in this corner, which is exactly what I should have done from the start.

It was rather hard for him to eat. I assumed he didn't eat the food they brought because he *couldn't*. With no hands, he had to bend forward and add weight to his nubs and bite into the food like some dog. His was practically eating from the ground. As for the drink…well, I helped him take a few sips. I didn't want to know how he managed to drink anything with no hands.

He rests on his back and then rolls over to his left side. "You know if this goes south, he'll kill you himself."

"I don't care."

"You're prepared to die?" His voice shifts, amused.

"I don't have anything else to lose. Death would be my pleasure." I wince as I tug on the zipper of the dress. It's chafing into my skin now.

"Just make sure you do it right."

"I will. You don't have to keep telling me."

Ronaldo rolls flat on his back and looks at me. His eyes are hard and serious, and without his hair on his face, he looks like a completely different person.

"If you get lucky and he decides to bring you in," he starts, sighing, "make sure you get me out of this place. I don't want to die in here. Don't forget about me."

I don't blink as our eyes hold. He has been through so much already. I don't know why he is here to begin with, but from what I know, I think he's learned his lesson. And it can't be as bad as being held captive and having your arms chopped off—suffering daily. No one deserves this kind of treatment but the men that put us in here. Ronaldo seems like a good guy. I'm sure whatever he did was a simple mistake that got blown out of proportion.

"I will," I whisper, stepping closer to him. "I promise."

We don't hear much until sunset.

It has been eerily quiet all day. Besides that one appearance from the white-haired man, none of them have come back to do their two-hour checks.

We didn't hear any loud laughing or boasting. Didn't smell any cigar smoke or microwaved noodles.

Today, things have shifted.

But it's as soon as the sun has set when we hear voices.

I perk up, clutching the knife in hand. There is one voice reporting something in Spanish. It's quick and deep. It sounds like the white-haired man.

Something creaks, and various amounts of footsteps are coming down the hallway. I'm not sure how many there are. It sounds like a lot of people, though.

With each of their steps, my heart is pounding in my chest.

Thu-thunk. Thu-thunk. Thu-thunk.

My sweaty palm is still wrapped around the knife, my eyes focused on the cell door. Ronaldo is in the very far corner, as far away from the door as possible.

The footsteps finally stop. I don't look up all the way, so all I see are their shoes through the iron bars. There are twelve sets. All of them are wearing black boots—all of them but one.

That one is wearing very expensive leather dress shoes.

Gradually, my line of sight pulls up, taking in the light brown dress pants covering strong, thick legs, and the black button-down shirt, barely hiding the strong arms and broad shoulders.

The first two buttons of the shirt are unbuttoned, revealing the top half of his firm chest. He's wearing a gold necklace with the crucifix hanging on the end.

Finally, I lock on his face. His chin is strong, jaw chiseled with light scruff; his full, pink lips are sculpted to perfection. His nose is straight, with a sharp angle and those eyes…

Those thin, dark-brown eyes are so hard to see through, yet they've ensnared me. I try to pull my vision away, but I can't. I'm stuck…and I don't know why.

I should hate this man—hate his face and how he stands much taller than the rest of the men with his lean, athletic build—but I can't seem to form hate while looking at him.

If I look away, though, I know I will hate him all over again.

He studies the cell very carefully, taking note of every small detail, but then he focuses on me. I know he can't really see me. It's not as bright in here as it once was.

"*Abrela*," he commands, accent heavy. *Open it.*

Axe Man steps forward to unlock the door. As soon as he does, he walks my way with heavy steps, grabs my arm, and yanks me up. He starts dragging me towards the boss, but I yank away before he can pull me out.

"Get off of me," I snarl, backing away.

Axe Man puts his eyes on me, grabbing my arm again and then slapping me with the back of his hand. "Stop fucking moving!"

"Calm the *fuck* down," the boss snaps, looking right at Axe Man.

Axe Man looks at the boss and pulls away from me. When he drops his hand, I snatch out the pocket knife, fling it open so that the blade is pointed at him, and then charge forward, screaming as I stab him right below the ribs.

He hollers out in pain, grabbing his side. The blade is jammed deep. Blood spills out, dripping down the handle of the knife and onto my fingers. I release it, staring at the pig, panting deep.

Two of the men behind the boss curse and then rush for me, dragging my body towards him. One of them has his hand clutched around the back of my neck. The other has my arms. My nostrils flare as I breathe unevenly, prepared for whatever is to follow.

The boss's demeanor hasn't changed. He isn't frowning or smiling. He isn't shocked or pleased. His face is just…blank. It reveals nothing whatsoever and for a split second, I think I'm fucked.

He steps towards me, narrowing his eyes. My dark hair has tumbled all over my face, covering me up. I can see him through the strands, clearly enough to know he's agitated.

"Why the fuck would you do that to one of my men, right in front of me?"

I don't respond to him. I'm too angry. Too heated.

He tilts my chin up so I can look at him fully. My hair slides back, and our eyes lock.

When he sees me, looks into my eyes, that's when his expression changes. He doesn't speak. He doesn't say a thing. His blank stare turns into one full of disbelief.

What the hell is he thinking?

This isn't the way I was expecting him to react at all. He seems...surprised to actually *see* me. As I stare back, I do find him familiar, but not familiar enough to ring a bell.

I feel like I've seen him before, but of course being in a cell for six days, being starved and dehydrated, can make one delusional.

Perhaps I was building up the idea of him so much that I felt like I knew him already.

"What the hell is her name?" he calls over his shoulder, still staring.

"We...don't know her first name, Jefe," the white-haired man responds in his native tongue.

"What is your fucking name?" he asks me in English, his voice gravelly.

"Gianna Nicotera," I spit at him. I know my father's name holds weight. I used to be afraid to share it, but if this man knew Toni, then he has to know who my father was.

His jaw clenches, and he finally snatches his eyes away from mine, stepping towards the white-haired man.

"She's a fucking *Nicotera*? Toni's new fucking wife is Gianna *fucking* Nicotera? Why the fuck didn't anyone tell me this shit?!"

"Because we didn't know, boss. We thought she was just Ricci or some bitch he found."

"Oh you didn't know?" He leans back, as if he's truly asking them this question. "So no one thought about doing a little research before bringing her onto my fucking property, huh?" He looks around as if someone will answer. "No? No one bothered?" He holds his hands out, leaving the question up in the air. They all remain tightlipped and still. "All right, then."

He smashes his lips together and strolls into the cell. He walks in leisurely, but as he does he's pulling something out of the pocket of his crisp, black shirt. He then turns at an angle.

"You watching this, green eyes?" he asks me.

I blink rapidly, utterly confused now. What the fuck is going on?

The boss steps closer to Axe Man, and I realize he has placed gold brass knuckles on his right hand.

"A few people made reports to me and they told me you pissed on her, Pico. You beat the shit out of her. And then you hit her again, right in my fucking face. Is it true what I'm hearing, Pico?"

"Please, Jefe, I didn't know who she was. I swear to God." Axe Man clings to the knife, bleeding out on the floor.

"You know what? I didn't expect you to know, Pico. I honestly didn't." He rolls his sleeves up as he says this. His movements are so slow and his voice is eerily calm. He takes one more step forward.

And then, out of nowhere, the boss becomes so livid that I hear his teeth chomp down and grit together.

The strands of his smooth, wavy hair flies everywhere as he yanks Axe Man up by the collar of his shirt, reels his arm back, and repeatedly punches him in the face.

I gasp sharply, jolting.

More blood gushes across the cell floor, and Axe Man groans as he falls, but the boss doesn't stop there.

He punches him again.

And again.

And again.

But, still, he doesn't stop.

He is relentless.

And his face is so casual with each blow that it terrifies me.

How can he not be showing any emotion—anger at least?

He doesn't quit punching until there is a puddle of blood surrounding Axe Man's face. When he brings himself upright, he's panting so hard and ragged that I shiver. He's like a raging bull that finally pinned the aggravating human on its back.

Deadly.

"You see what happened?" the boss asks, huffing. "*This* is what fucking happens when you don't know your shit around here. If you don't keep yourself up to date—go that extra fucking mile to make sure shit like this doesn't happen—then you will get fucked up. Just like this piece of shit right here!" He looks at all of the men standing in the hallway and then he drops Axe Man.

Axe man collapses on top of the pocketknife, but he barely moves. He groans and blood gushes out of his mouth, seeping down the corner, over his chin.

The boss snatches out the handkerchief from the pocket of his shirt to wipe off the brass knuckles. He then slides the brass knuckles back into his pocket, tossing the handkerchief at the Axe Man.

"Now get cleaned up, you sloppy piece of shit. You're getting your blood all over the fucking floor."

The boss's eyes swing over to me and he walks casually in my direction, as if nothing ever even happened.

Horrified, I lower my gaze to the bloody man on the floor. His face is butchered, and he still has the blade jammed inside of him. For a split second, I feel terrible for ever putting it there.

But then I remember him urinating on me, beating me senseless, and starving me. He deserves this. Actually…no. He deserves far worse than this.

"Let's not be so fucking stupid next time. Do you all understand me?" the boss demands.

"Sí, Jefe," they all say in unison.

"Bueno. Patanza!" he shouts. The woman that let me go to the bathroom walks through the crowd of men.

"Sí, Jefe?"

"Take her up to the mansion. Put her in a nice room and make sure she is showered, fed, and in la *arte galería* a las nueve. No later." I assume he says this in English so I won't think I'm being dragged off to meet my doom.

Patanza looks me over, flaring her nostrils. "Sí, Jefe." She walks forward and all of the men step back to let her through. "Come on," she commands lightly.

She walks down the hallway and I start to walk with her, but not before looking back at the boss.

He's already watching me, his face smooth—clear of emotion. His dark eyes hold mine as I scurry down the hallway, and he doesn't let up until I'm at the door that Patanza is holding open.

I decide to look away first. I know he won't, plus I shouldn't do anything to further upset him. Not after witnessing what just happened.

When I've met up to Patanza, she shuts the door behind me and I follow her through the cramped gray room.

There are small screens on one of the walls across from me, and on one of them I see the boss and the rest of the men standing in the hallway. He is pointing fingers and shouting at each of them.

I'm surprised it's in my defense.

There were cameras in there the whole time?

How in the hell didn't I notice?

I spot Ronaldo on another screen and he's sitting in the corner, trying to hide in the shadows. Now I believe him when he said the boss is crazy. I believe that the boss really did that to him.

What I saw in that cell was inhumane. It was scary—a good cause for nightmares.

Patanza leads the way towards a tall brown door and pushes it open.

"Keep up," she snaps.

I pick up my pace, delighted to be outside again. Freedom rings, but only for a short while. I do myself the liberty of enjoying this moment. My friends, the gulls, caw loudly, as if they've been awaiting my presence.

I inhale the salty air, and then I look towards the beach. It is just as I imagined—if not, better. The turquoise water is clear, shimmering beneath the pinkish sky.

The sand is white—almost spotless. The setting sun is breathtaking. It's been so long since I've seen it.

"Where are we?" I ask.

"Don't ask any fucking questions. Just because this is happening, it doesn't make us friends or you in the fucking clear. He's not done with you."

I stare at her, focused on the long, black hair beneath her black cap and the dimples on her lower back. The clothes she wears... How can she wear them around these brutes? Belly shirts and low riding camouflage pants. I wonder if she's always been a bitch. Why the hell does she even work for him?

She's the only woman I've seen down there, and she's not ugly at all. She's stunning, really. How can she stomach any of what we just saw?

When we walk up a set of stone steps, I see the mansion come into view. It's made of a cream-colored stucco, the roof dark, offsetting the overall appearance.

It is so amazing that I almost stop walking just to take it all in.

Gold spotlights illuminate the house from the ground, revealing it for what it truly is.

A beautiful residence.

We walk across a short wooden bridge, and there is a garden of various colored frangipani flowers that look like they have recently bloomed. I can smell them from where we are. Sweet and fresh.

As I study each aspect of this home, I wonder how a man like him can live in such a lovely place. Surely he doesn't deserve any of this.

Not after knowing what he does to people in those cells.

Not after witnessing him switch from rational to a complete maniac in a matter of seconds.

Patanza enters a code on the box at the gate and when it buzzes open, she walks past a wide, oblong shaped pool. A small waterfall drifts down from the far corner of it, the lounge chairs decorated in white and black cushions.

She jogs up the steps and reaches for the doorknob. Once the door is open I'm greeted by a large chrome and black kitchen.

There is an older woman standing in front of the oven, waiting for something to finish baking.

She looks over and frowns at Patanza. Patanza rolls her eyes, muttering, "This way," to me before looking away.

The woman sees me and her eyes grow wide. She's older, with her silver and black hair pulled up into a tight bun, and a sharp nose, just like the boss's.

"Patanza, who is this?" she asks. "And why is she covered in so much blood?"

"I don't know," Patanza snips. "Ask Jefe."

The woman thins her eyes at Patanza before looking at me again. I pick up my pace, knowing it's best to keep walking. I know I look and smell hideous right now. I definitely don't look like I belong in a home like this.

I look down and there is fresh blood on me. First Toni's blood was on my dress and now Axe Man's blood is.

Jesus.

We are up the stairs before I know it. Patanza walks down the hallway and

PASSION & VENOM

takes a left. We pass six doors before she finally stops and grabs a doorknob. She pushes it open and then walks in.

I cautiously follow her inside. When she steps back and looks towards the bed, I know she won't try anything. She's no fool. She won't disobey her boss's orders.

"Clothes are in the closet. All sizes, so you should find something that fits you. Soap and shampoo is in the bathroom. When you're finished, I'll be waiting out in the hallway so you can eat. You have two hours to do all of this before we meet Jefe. Better make them fucking count. They may be your last."

She smirks on her way out the door.

I watch her leave. Does she think she's intimidating me? My father received death threats and warrants for breakfast. This isn't anything new.

One thing Daddy taught me was to never fear a woman. A woman will always carry some sort of emotion. A woman is much easier to manipulate and much more lenient than a man. When Patanza told Axe Man to let me come out and pee, that was her femininity showing.

When the door is shut completely, I turn back around and take in the bedroom. The bedspread is turquoise and white. It's a beautiful, unique design, with a sheer white canopy that can't be beat. I walk towards it and start to touch it, but then I remember the blood on my hands.

Seeing it makes me cringe, and my stomach forms in knots.

It's not my blood, and it has to go.

I hurry to the bathroom. The walls are made of white and blue tile, the shower as well, the glass clean and inviting. I walk towards it, but on my way in I can't help but take a glance at the mirror.

I stop dead in my tracks.

Deep, dark circles have formed around my eyes from lack of sleep. My hair is frizzy and matted, and there's a red splotch on my forehead, where I hit my head when Axe Man gave me a beating from hell.

My lips are so raw and chapped that I see the blood between the cracks. I lick them and it burns. My wedding day makeup has run down my cheeks. I look dead already.

But that's not the worst of it.

The worst is my dress.

My beautiful wedding gown.

It's torn.

Bloody.

Ragged.

It's no longer ivory. It's smeared in dirt, oil, grime, urine, and way too much blood.

I snatch my gaze away, tears forming at the rim of my eyelids. I start the shower and strip out of my dress immediately. I keep watch of my surroundings as I wash.

I may be getting treated humanely now, but I don't know what's in store for later.

The steam fills my pores and I stand beneath the stream, soaking up the water, making sure every single part of me is thoroughly cleaned—every part but my still-raw wrists.

I think about what Ronaldo said in that cell, about making the *king* notice.

I think I did the job.

If I hadn't stabbed Axe Man, he wouldn't have given two shits about me. It probably would have been me getting the beating instead. I hate that my violence led him to his, though.

After my shower, I grab one of the fluffy, white towels on the handle bar and wrap it around my body. I rub my hair dry with a smaller towel and then walk out of the bathroom, peeking around the corner.

When I know no one is around, I tiptoe to the closet, across the soft, tan carpet.

Flipping the light switch, I step inside and when the closet is illuminated, I am stunned.

Patanza wasn't kidding. There are clothes of every size here. Some look worn, but most of it is new.

I take down a pair of jeans my size, a long-sleeved gray shirt, and some tennis shoes.

I walk back to the bathroom and stare into the mirror. Normally, I'd do my hair, makeup—all of it. There is a jewelry box on the shelf beside the mirror, but I won't use any of this stuff. It's not mine, and I am not a puppet they can toy with.

I do decide to use the bandages they have to wrap my wrists, in hopes that they'll continue to heal without getting infected. I hiss and stomp as I pour the alcohol on each one before wrapping them.

Besides that, nothing else matters. I'll let my hair air dry and walk around with purplish bruises around my eyes. That way he'll know just how much damage I incurred because of him. Because of *his* people.

I walk to the door, pulling it open slowly.

Patanza is standing in the hallway like she said she would be. Her hands are behind her back, her brows dipped as she focuses on me.

"It's about damn time," she mutters, pushing off the wall. "Let's go. You have less than an hour."

"Do I really?" I ask as I walk quicker.

She looks over her shoulder but doesn't respond.

Instead, she marches down the stairs, and I follow her lead. I take in the portraits on the walls. There are four of them. All of them have a different man on them. All of the men have straight faces and cold, dead eyes.

It almost feels like they're watching me.

I don't know why, but the sight of the portraits sends me chills. I assume they are the boss's ancestors.

When we make it downstairs, Patanza makes a right. I frown as I look to the left where the kitchen is.

"I thought you said we were going to eat?"

"We are."

She doesn't look back. She continues walking. Warily, I follow her, keeping watch of my surroundings. I don't realize how nervous I am until I feel my fingernails digging into my palms.

I loosen my tightened fists as we walk down a long corridor. There are more portraits on the walls, but they aren't of people. They are paintings.

All beautiful.

Clearly masculine.

Dark and chilling.

There is a signature at the bottom of each one. A large D and some scribble.

As I study each one we pass, I realize the same person has created them all. One of them of a young boy bent over catches me off guard.

The others were scenery photos but this one is gritty and sad.

The boy is bent over, staring down at his bloody hands. In front of him is a sea, but it's not a normal blue one. It's crimson, the waves high. A village surrounds the boy. He seems pained…in agony.

I don't blink as I stare at it. The main thing that gets me is the blood on his hands—as if he did something he never should have done.

"Let's go." Patanza's agitated voice slices through my thoughts and I blink rapidly, hurrying after her.

When we are at the end of the corridor, she opens two white french doors and walks in. Inside the room is a dining table. This table can seat at least twenty people.

In the middle of the table, on the left side, there is a place already set up. A silver tray has been placed there, and I can smell the food from where I stand.

Salty.

Sweet.

Savory.

My mouth waters and the urge to shove Patanza out of the way just to get to the food seizes me, but I maintain control. I don't want to look desperate or greedy.

She shuts the door behind us and then steps to the far corner. "Go. Eat." She lifts a hand, gesturing to the covered tray.

I side-eye her before going for the food. With each step, I'm taking in the set-up of the dining room. The high ceilings and large chandeliers make it appear elegant, but the portrait on the wall across from the door is what throws it off scale.

It's a portrait of the boss. It's like the others along the stairwell. His face is serious, his jaw locked, but unlike their eyes, his aren't as dark or cold.

His brown irises swim with confidence and wickedness, yes, but there is also something else there.

I can't exactly put my finger on it, but I know it isn't a bad thing.

I pull the chair out slowly and it scrapes the floor. My eyes flicker up to Patanza. Hers are narrowed, watching me very carefully.

I sit down and slide the wooden chair in, studying the domed serving tray. I look to the right and there is only a spoon. It's plastic.

I look up at her again and a smirk is on her lips, but she's no longer looking at me. Her arms are locked tight over her chest.

No knives or forks. I'm glad they are taking me seriously.

I lift a hand and take off the lid. A waft of steam runs across my face and the mouth-watering increases. There's baked chicken, broccoli, and a sweet potato with butter and cinnamon inside of it.

My insides are in a frenzy now. My belly rumbles with joy. I pick up the spoon and immediately dig into the potato. The smooth, sweet taste sweeps over my taste buds and I shut my eyes for a brief moment, sighing.

It's good.

So good.

I dig into the broccoli with my hands, leaving the spoon standing in the sweet potato. My teeth bite into the chicken, snatching off a piece and chewing quickly. Bite after bite seems to only get better.

I've had way better meals than this, but it's been six days since the last time I've had a decent one, minus the protein-filled breakfast given to us this morning. I moan as I eat more of the sweet potato.

A door across from me opens up rapidly and a tall, young man walks in with a pitcher in one hand, a cup in the other.

I pause on digging into the chicken, swallowing the chunk that's already in my mouth. He looks at me with quirked brows, moving quickly as he meets at my side.

"Té?" He places the cup down and lifts the pitcher of iced tea in the air.

I bob my head. "Yes, please."

He pours away and I pick it up quickly, guzzling it down. When I've finished, he pours another, but I take note of his stunned expression.

I can't believe I'm being so barbaric, but for all I know this could be my last meal. My last day. Like Patanza said, I better make it count.

What the hell, right?

"Thank you," I breathe, smiling crookedly as I place my half-empty glass down.

He simply nods his head, topping my drink off before walking back out of the dining room. I catch the look he gives Patanza and she shakes her head, laughing silently.

They're mocking me.

I couldn't care less.

I finish my meal in a matter of minutes. By the time I'm done, all that's left is the peel of the potato, specks of green from the broccoli, and the bare bones of the chicken.

Patanza pushes off the wall and flicks her wrist. "Clean yourself up," she mutters as she steps closer.

I grab the hand towel that was beneath the tray and wipe off, pushing out of my chair and standing as I do. I toss the towel down and then step over, looking towards the french doors. A shadow appears. Someone is coming.

Patanza notices me looking and turns around to look at the door.

The tall, skinny man with white hair from the cells walks in and looks from me to her with a ticking jaw. "She done?"

"Yes."

"Good. He wants to see her now." The white-haired man looks me over in my new clothes. His eyes broil with lust. I snatch my gaze away, staring at the tips of my shoes.

"Okay. We're coming," Patanza states.

"No." He holds a hand up and she stops in her tracks. "He asked *me* to bring her."

She thins her eyes at him for a moment. Then she looks from him to me. Stepping back, she gestures towards the tall man and I press my lips together, trudging forward.

He steps back, allowing me to walk past, and I feel him looking right at my ass as I do.

I hear Patanza scoff but not much else. The man slams the door behind him and then steps around me, licking his lips.

"This way." He walks down a darker hallway. There are lamps on, but it's darker, not as bright as the corridor with the paintings.

His heavy boots squish on the marble floor and my sneakers squeak as I try to keep up. We walk for what feels like two whole minutes before we finally reach a staircase that goes down. He hustles down the steps and I take them one-by-one, my thumb rubbing over my wedding ring.

Two brown double doors appear at the end of the hallway when I make it down. The tall man meets up to it and knocks twice. I stay at least five steps away from him.

"*Adelante*!" The boss's voice rises and the tall man opens the door right away. He flicks his fingers for me to follow.

My mouth feels dryer, but I follow him in. Slowly.

When the door is shut behind me, I look towards the boss. His hands are behind his back as he stands in front of a blank, white canvas. Above the canvas is another portrait hung on the wall. It's way bigger than the rest I've seen. In fact, every portrait inside this room is.

The walls are a dark brown color. On the wall to my right, there is a two-seater sofa. To my left, a single black chair. The ceiling is tan and vaulted with spotlights hanging from them, shining on each creation.

A staircase is across from him. A tall table between us.

I look up, and see more paintings above, a bed with a headboard, and candles. A violin is on a stand up there, and my brows dip at the sight of it. For some reason that violin just doesn't fit in here…and neither do I.

Mom used to play violin. She was really good at it, too. She tried to teach me but I never had the patience for it. I did love listening, though. I loved to be entertained. That's probably the reason I've been caught in a jam such as this one.

Toni was my entertainment. He made me laugh, swoon, and cry. My eyes burn as I think of Toni. And then I focus on the boss with a scowl.

"Leave us," the boss commands.

The tall man turns quickly and walks out, shutting the heavy doors behind him.

I rub my thumb across the ring again, the thick cut diamond. The boss picks up a small black container and walks to a sink behind the staircase that I didn't previously notice.

He runs the water, filling the container, and then comes back. After placing it down, he rolls up the sleeves of his shirt. I just realized that he's changed clothes. He's now wearing a white button-down. It's much more revealing. His arms are thick and definitely sculpted.

Raking a hand through his sleek hair, he finally turns to look at me. His firm gaze travels over the length of my body, and when he sees my outfit, he glowers.

"You have a full wardrobe of dresses, skirts, blouses…but you decide to wear jeans and a regular shirt. Strike one."

"What the hell does that mean?" I ask boldly.

He places his hands behind his back again, pacing the area near the canvas slowly.

"You have questions. Lots of them," he notes. "Well, let me start off by telling you my name. Most call me Jefe. My real name is Draco Molina. But I suppose you can call me...*sir*." He flashes a wicked smile.

"How did you know I was a Nicotera?"

He looks up, a spark in his eye, his lips flat. "I just knew." He faces the canvas again.

"You knew my father?"

He turns halfway, glancing over his shoulder. "I knew him well, yes."

I debate on whether I should ask my next question. The truth is I'm afraid to know the answer. If I know, then I'll definitely know my fate.

"Was..." I release a ragged sigh. "Was he an enemy of yours?"

He frowns at the statement, turning around to face me completely. "If he was my enemy, do you think you'd still be alive, standing in front of me in clothes that I bought and food in your belly that I told my cooks to make?" He shakes his head, wagging a finger. "I am not your enemy, little girl."

I narrow my eyes. "You *are* my enemy."

"Excuse me?"

"You had my husband killed!"

He lets out a bitter chuckle. "You mean Trigger Toni? Yeah, I had him killed. It was a personal order, in fact, and it needed to be done."

His smugness is like a stab in the gut and the heart. I grimace as I storm forward, rushing around the tall art table. All of my morals are lost, my rage on full display. I stop just in time to save myself. I don't get too close to touch him. Just close enough to really see him.

His tan skin is clear of any markings or scars. His lips are fuller than I thought. Pink. His eyelashes are long and thick.

His eyes flash with an amount of intimidation I've never seen before. He inclines a brow, his glare telling me to choose wisdom over stupidity.

It would be dumb of me to hurt or threaten him, but I need answers. Now.

"Why?" I demand.

"Why what?"

"Why did you have my husband killed?"

He folds his arms. "He was a liar. A pig. A rabid animal that needed to be put down, gently or not. He was a murderer—"

"Yeah, and so are you!"

His face changes. He drops his arms and steps forward with flared nostrils and a clenched jaw. "Watch your fucking tone around me, little girl. I allowed you into my home. Show some goddamn respect."

"Respect the man who left me alone with those brutes? Why should I?" I challenge, and I am terribly afraid of his answer.

He looks me over before locking eyes with me again. "Because if you don't, I won't be so keen to let you live. Having you here burdens me more than it aids me. Don't make me end up breaking your precious little neck."

And he could, with hands his size. My petite frame is no match for him, no matter how bold I want to be right now.

My lips smash together. I step back several steps and fold my arms tightly over my chest. "I'd rather be dead than in the same home of the man that killed my husband."

"Oh really?" He scowls. "Then go. But don't expect my protection. It won't be easy finding your way out of here, but even if you do manage to escape, the damage that'll be done to you will be beyond repair. While you are here, under my fucking roof, no one touches you. But when you're out of my hands…well…" He flashes a devilish smile. "…I don't give a fuck what happens to you then, *niñita*."

An eerie smirk sweeps across his full lips. He's so full of himself and it truly grates my nerves.

As badly as I want to run, I can't. Not until I figure out where the hell I am and actually have a plan to back myself up. For all I know, we're in the middle of nowhere—on an island or something. It has to be the right time. Anything could happen to me.

I'm surrounded by ignorant pigs and their grimy thoughts. I know it's ironic to say, but the boss seems like the most decent of them all…but no kindness now will ever be able to make up for what he's done.

"Can I go back to the room?" I ask, and hate that my voice cracks.

"Go." He turns his back to me, picking up a paintbrush from the cup on the stand.

I turn rapidly, and rush for the door with cloudy vision. My anger has blinded me tenfold.

Before I can open the door, the boss calls after me, and what he calls me causes a gasp to spill through my parted lips. It's not *niñita* or *green eyes*.

"Gianna Nicotera," he says, as if he's familiar with my name. The way it rolls off his tongue—his accent enhancing the sound of it—makes me wonder if I know this man at all. He seems familiar, but I can't place it.

He's not too much older than I am.

I glance over my shoulder at him. His back is still facing me, his fingertips running along the fine wooden handle of his paintbrush.

"Breakfast is at eight a.m. sharp. Be on time or you will regret it. I don't admire tardiness."

I don't give a shit what he admires. He doesn't own or control me. Fucking bastard.

I snatch the door open and storm out, but the tall man calls after me from his corner, quickly shaking his head. "I take you back. You don't walk freely around here, bitch. Not until he says so."

I feel my right eye twitch when he calls me that, but there isn't much I can do. As of now I am trapped here and from the looks of it, there is nowhere to run.

I saw how Patanza had to get in here. There are codes. Gates. There is no escape unless you are given permission to go...or unless you work for him.

But even so, there is nothing but darkness surrounding the idea of freedom.

I won't get out clean—or probably alive.

He made it simple in there.

If I run, I die.

I stare at the bedroom door.

I feel the presence there.

Someone is watching.

Waiting.

I saw their footsteps go past and they haven't gone back. I pull the blanket up to my nose, still staring at the door.

I don't know if he has someone on guard around my door, but if they were being a guard, they wouldn't have passed so quietly. So *sinisterly*.

The hallway light shuts out behind the door. It's completely dark where the crack is. Pitch black.

I turn on my side with an intense glare on the doorknob.

It jiggles gently and I gasp, covering myself up some more—until I feel like I've drowned beneath the thick blanket.

The jiggling stops.

All is quiet.

All I hear are my ragged breaths.

And then I hear them.

The same footsteps that I almost thought I had imagined. They move across in slow, measured strides and I listen until I can no longer hear them.

Sighing, I turn onto my back and stare up at the canopy. I don't feel safe here. I am being forced to sleep with one eye open.

I don't even trust my life in his hands. He said I wouldn't be harmed here, but how can I believe any of what he says after the way he killed my husband?

I don't trust him and he doesn't trust me. Why keep me here if he knows I will just be a burden…

Unless he thinks I know something—but there isn't much to tell. Toni kept his work life out of our personal life unless it was completely necessary to tell me.

I guess he didn't think this Draco Molina would be a threat worth discussing.

I'd never heard of this man before now. I don't know who he is and even if I did know something I would never tell that son-of-a-bitch.

DAY SEVEN

he sunlight is spread across my body. My curtains have been opened by someone, but I don't know who…that is, until I see the woman sitting in the recliner across from the end of the bed.

I sit up rapidly with a sharp gasp. She has her legs folded, her brown hair tucked neatly behind her ears. Her white suit is crisp and clean, the silky red blouse beneath it revealing most of her cleavage.

Her brunette hair swims around her shoulders, a small smirk on her lips. I notice there are honey streaks in her hair.

I yank the blanket up to my chest, sliding my back against the headboard as I stare at her. "Who the hell are you?"

"No one to fear." Her ruby red lips purse together, and then she uncrosses her legs to stand. She walks towards my window, running her fingers along the white curtain. "I decorated this room, you know?" She looks over her shoulder. "Draco let me."

PASSION & VENOM

I don't say anything. I just study her. Though she seems well put together, there is something off about her. Her eyes are dark. There is no happiness within them. But what really catches me off guard are the scars around her ankles, like she's been bound by them before. Her ankles are exactly how my wrists will be once healed.

"Why are you in here?" I demand. "This is my room."

"Oh, don't get so full of yourself, honey. This was once my room too, and a girl named Nilah, but she wasn't very compliant." Her arms fold across her chest as she looks me over. "You know what happens to the girls Draco tries to save, but they turn out to be disobedient?"

I narrow my eyes.

"They end up *dead*."

"Why are you telling me this?"

"I just want you to know. I heard there was a new girl here. One that Draco didn't want being touched. I also heard that you got loud with him last night in his galería which wasn't very wise on your behalf." She shakes her head with disapproval. "I am surprised he didn't do anything to you."

She walks around my bed and to the door. "But I guess this morning will make up for that."

"What do you mean?" I ask quickly.

Her eyes spark, as if she's pleased to know what I don't. "You missed breakfast. Draco has a strict code. Everyone must be in the dining room for breakfast by eight and at dinner before seven and no later."

"I don't even know what time it is right now. I don't have a clock in here."

She shrugs one shoulder. "That's why you wake up and figure it out yourself. Sleep in the dining room if you have to. Doesn't matter as long as you're on time."

She starts to walk out but I scramble out of bed, calling after her.

She pauses, peering over her shoulder at me.

"What is he going to do to me?"

She looks me over in my shorts and baggy T-shirt, shaking her head with displeasure once again. "Look at you. Trying to hide your blessings beneath that shirt. When he tells you he'll protect you under his watch, he means it. Don't insult him."

I frown. "That doesn't answer my question." I know she's trying to find anything to criticize me about. Maybe that's why she's here so early. So she can see me in my ugliest form, with drool on my chin and knotted hair. So she can see me before I decide to primp myself.

She sighs, removing her hand from the doorknob. "He won't touch you, if that's what you're thinking." Then she grins. "But he will be sure to make you remember to never be late again."

The way she says it sends goosebumps running down my arms and spine. How can this possibly flatter her? He had to have rescued her in some way.

Ronaldo said only people that he wants to call him by his real name can call him that. I figure the person has to be close to him or family. She's clearly not family...so does it make them a couple?

Is she his whore?

I rush forward and slam the door and then lean against it as I stare out of the window. I can see the ocean from where I stand. It's glorious this morning...but all this beauty is a façade.

All of this beauty represents lies. On the outside it may seem marvelous, but inside all you will sense is fear, lies, and even death.

I walk to the closet and decide to wear something a little nicer. I can't walk around here looking like the desperate, scared girl. I have a backbone and I plan on using it.

There is a yellow dress I find as I skim through. It has bowties on the back, stops below the knee. I dress in it quickly, and then walk to the bathroom to brush my teeth and then my hair.

My chapped lips are starting to bother me. I pick up the petroleum jelly and rub some on my lips. Walking back to the closet, I take down a pair of sandals and slide into them.

I check the mirror.

I look alive, to say the least.

It's decent enough.

I walk to the door and pull it open. The hallway is clear so I make my way down. I hear pots and pans clanking, so I walk to the kitchen. Surely there's a clock in there somewhere.

As soon as I make it down the staircase and to the kitchen, all of the maids stop working. They focus on me, studying my dress and especially my hair. Immediately, they start speaking Spanish, rambling on about a million things they probably think I don't understand.

"Late." Someone bumps into me from behind and when I see Patanza walk around with a cup in her hand, I scowl.

She shoves the cup into one of the maid's hands and then folds her arms. My eyes bounce over her to check the clock on the wall.

"It's only 8:30," I state.

"Doesn't matter. Late is late. Jefe doesn't like it."

"So…what does that mean?"

She shakes silently with laughter, and some of the maids avoid my eyes when I ask that. "You'll find out."

She walks around me, but before she can go, she says, "Oh, and dinner is at 7 p.m. sharp. No later."

Yeah, I know that. "Do you think I can get a clock in the room I'm in or something?"

Patanza stares at me as if I've lost my mind, and then she starts laughing so hard that I cringe. "Wow," she laughs again. She looks towards the maids while pointing a mocking thumb at me. "Can you believe this bitch? She's just released from the cages and she's already making requests. Fucking bold."

The maids frown at Patanza before looking at me uncertainly. They are all confused. I don't think they speak much English.

Patanza walks off quickly and I watch her open a door and shut it behind her. I look down at the floor, but when I feel eyes on me, I turn rapidly to look at the maids.

Startled, they jump right back into their work—scrubbing the counters, sweeping the floors, and washing the dishes.

I make way towards the dining room, down the long corridor. The french doors appear and I rush for them, pushing them open rapidly. The room is empty, but there is still food on the table.

One of the butlers picks up a silver tray at the end of the table and when he sees me walking in, he lifts a brow.

Heels click along the floor from a distance and then the young woman that was in my room not too long ago walks in from what I assume is another kitchen. I hear dishes clanking and people talking.

She slows her pace as she spots me, looking me over in my new attire.

She doesn't make a disgusted face. She looks surprised.

"Can I eat?" I ask softly.

She scrutinizes me briefly before pointing her gaze to the table. She then looks at the butler who has a few dirty dishes in hand and murmurs something to him in Spanish.

The butler nods and then takes off, whistling in cue as he enters the kitchen.

Before I know it, at least four more men come out and collect the food that's on the table. They grab the empty bowls, plates, and silverware but I rush forward before they can escape.

"Hey—wait!" I shout, but they merely ignore my plea, heading towards the kitchen without so much as a glance my way. "What the fuck!" I snap at her. "What did you tell them? I haven't eaten yet!"

She picks up a biscuit from the last tray on the table. "You aren't supposed to."

"What?" My voice is laced with utter disbelief.

I shove past her and pick up a biscuit. She smacks it out of my hand and then picks up the tray. "You aren't supposed to eat," she bites. "If he finds out you've eaten on my watch, he'll punish me too."

"I don't care. Starving me is cruelty," I seethe, rubbing the back of my hand. "I didn't know what time it was."

"Get used to it." Her eyes drop down to my chest and I back away, folding my arms.

She trots around the table and into the kitchen. When she's gone, I stare down at the empty table. There are only crumbs left, and my heart cracks in my chest.

Tears blind me, but I won't stick around here for them to see.

This is bullying. Pure ignorance. I twist around and storm out of the dining room, but due to my lack of attention, I run right into a sculpted, broad chest.

PASSION & VENOM

Large hands grip my upper arms, and I gasp as I look up and meet familiar, dark brown eyes.

Draco.

I yank out of his oddly gentle grasp, scowling up at him.

His face remains even, his lips meshing together.

"I didn't get to eat," I say without thinking.

"I don't admire tardiness," he informs me again, and then he steps around me, continuing his walk down the hallway. I watch him descend the hall and take the staircase down that leads to his art room. Not once does he look back at me.

My heart pounds erratically in my chest. Sniffling, I swipe my face before running down the hallway and up the stairs. There are maids and butlers around, but none of them look me in the face.

I bet they are trained to ignore stuff like this.

A lonely, desperate woman basically crying out for help. I go past six doors and burst into the seventh bedroom. This is the safest place as of now...but for how long?

When will he take this from me too?

I won't be like that bitch that was here this morning. I won't appreciate any of this. I won't cater to that demonic man.

All he has done is taken from me. His men have abused me, and now he's starving me.

Shit, he won't have to protect me for long. Before we know it, I'll be dead trying to make it out alive.

God.

I just want to go home.

To my surprise, an alarm clock is delivered to my room. Unfortunately, the tall, skinny man with the white hair is the deliverer.

"Here." He drops it on the bed, standing close, looking at my bare legs. "Plug it in."

I look down at the alarm clock. It's black with silver buttons. Picking it up, I stand and turn for the nightstand. There is an outlet behind it, so I pull the stand forward a bit to reach it.

As I bend down, I feel him looking at my ass. He's so close to me. My heartbeat accelerates, and not in a good way. I jam the plug into the outlet and then pull back, standing up straight and backing away.

"What time is it?" I ask, tilting my chin and gesturing towards his watch.

A smile twitches at the corners of his lips. "How about you find out for yourself." He grabs my tender wrist and yanks me forward. His rough hands run up my forearm and I nearly stop breathing as his face comes in closer.

I focus on the floor. Bringing his wrist up, he says, "Look."

My eyes drift down to the black leather watch. I take note of the time and then pull away from him, turning around and punching it into the alarm clock. I sit slowly, and he chuckles beneath his breath.

"Stupid bitch," he grumbles in Spanish. "I don't know why he's saving you. Would be smarter to just pass you around and then *sell* you." His heavy boots clomp across the floor and then he stops at the door. In English he says, "He doesn't want you at dinner. Don't come out until breakfast tomorrow." With that, the door slams behind him and he's gone.

The heavy atmosphere is sucked back out, but only some of it.

It's still not safe.

Three steps.

Three footsteps are what it takes this person to go past my door and wait there. I don't know what they're waiting for. Frankly, I'm too afraid to go out and check. It might be the man with the white hair.

Or maybe it's Axe Man lurking around, seeking revenge.

With a beating like that, I wouldn't be surprised if he lost all respect for Draco. I haven't seen him since the cells. I wonder if he's even alive.

I check the alarm clock.

2:08 a.m.

They wait there for nearly ten minutes, and with each minute my heart is pounding like a drum.

And then…with three simple steps, the person is past my door and walking down the hallway. I don't hear the steps again for the rest of the night.

DAY EIGHT

I *woke up at 7 a.m.*

It is now 7:40 and I'm done getting ready. The short-sleeved blue dress I'm wearing is ironed. My hair has been French-braided down to the middle of my back, and my lips are glossed.

He can't say I'm late today. I'm ready.

I collect all of the items I used from the bathroom counter and put them back in their places. When the bathroom is clean, I walk back out and make the bed. I glance at the alarm clock as I do. I have eight minutes to make it.

And I will.

I toss the pillows on and then I'm out of the door. I trot down the marble staircase with a great feeling. I can't describe it, but I'm glad to be on top of things this morning.

I was hungry as hell last night and I still am today. I need food and I need it badly.

PASSION & VENOM

I can smell the breakfast as I walk down the hallway. The aromas are fresh and warm.

The french doors are already open so I walk right through them, but I immediately come to a halt as I spot Draco sitting at the head of the table, opposite of where I stand.

The young woman that I just met yesterday is two seats down from him and on the other side, right beside him, is the older woman I saw in the kitchen when Patanza first brought me here.

Draco has both arms on the armrest of his chair. His chair is much bigger than the rest of them. It's almost like a throne, made of burgundy and black leather.

He tilts a brow as his eyes wander up and down my frame. He starts from my head and carries his gaze down to my feet. The older woman stares at me with utter confusion while the young woman from yesterday tries to act like I'm not even present.

I hesitate as I walk forward, unsure of where to sit. I don't want to sit too close, so I take a seat near the end of the table.

"No." Draco's deep voice rises as I start to pull the chair out. My eyes dart over to him. "Closer."

I inhale and exhale slowly, walking past a few more chairs. When I'm at least three away from the younger woman, I pull it out and it screeches across the hardwood.

Draco watches me closely, rubbing the pad of his thumb and forefinger together. There is a thick, silver ring on his pinky finger with the shape of a skull on it.

I slide the chair in and rest my hands in my lap. A roman numerals clock is on the wall to my right and I watch the big hand tick by.

Only three more minutes until eight o' clock.

When those three minutes are up, several butlers in black button down shirts and gloves walk out with domed trays in hand. They place one down in front of each of us, while one of them comes around to fill our glasses up with orange juice.

When the butler's have done their jobs, Draco bobs his head and they all take off—all but one. The butler that stays, stands near the entryway of the kitchen with his fingers folded in front of him. His eyes are fixed on the wall across and nothing else. His orders, I presume.

Draco takes off the lid covering his meal and places it down. The older and younger woman follow suit, and I do as well.

There are strips of bacon, scrambled eggs, toast with small silver containers of jelly, and orange slices.

Everyone else has already dug into his or her meals while I look over mine. My mouth waters as their forks scrape and clink on the china.

The older woman starts to talk to Draco in Spanish and he responds dully, chewing thoroughly. I pick up my fork and dig it into the eggs.

But it's as I bring it to my mouth that Draco straightens his back, his eyebrows drawing together.

"Did I say you could eat?" His voice comes out deep and heavy.

Both women look at me. He glares at the fork that's halfway to my mouth. I swallow the lump in my throat, lowering the fork.

"Oh…I thought…"

"You thought what?" he bellows. "That you were in the fucking clear?" His head shakes and he drops his fork to pick up his orange juice. "Put the fucking fork down and put the lid back over the food."

I don't dare blink as he picks up his juice, his eyes locked on me. I drop the fork with shaky hands, picking up the lid to cover the breakfast.

I stare down at the silver dome—at my stretched reflection. I feel the older woman looking at me, but she continues eating. The younger woman doesn't bother looking my way.

"You were late yesterday," Draco proclaims.

"I didn't have a clock. I didn't know what time it was."

I avoid his eyes, but I feel his hot glare on the side of my face. Through the corner of my eye I see him place his glass down and then pick up his fork to take a bite of his eggs.

"You met Francesca?" he questions, looking at the younger woman and then at me again.

I nod.

"I didn't hear you. Speak when I ask you a question."

I look up and his jaw pulses. "Yes, I met her."

"I hope she made you feel welcomed."

I side-eye her. "Sure." Dropping my head, I focus on my fingernails. I am so humiliated. I feel hot all over. My body is broiling with rage.

"Gianna," Draco murmurs, and I look up rapidly. He has a fist on the table, his head cocked. "How did your breakfast look? Appetizing?"

I nod, but then I quickly respond. "Yes."

"Do you want it?"

"Yes."

"I bet you do. The smell of this crispy bacon and buttery toast is making your belly growl with hunger. You're dying for a taste…and you could have had some if you'd only been on time yesterday morning." When I drop my head, he demands me to look up at him again. His face is straight now, his eyes as hard as stone. "You're going to watch us eat and then when we are done, you will gather all of the dishes and take them into that kitchen over there." He points towards the hall the butler is standing near. "Is that understood?"

I nod reluctantly. "Yes."

"Yes, what?"

"Yes…sir."

"That's good, *niñita*."

"Little girl?" Francesca asks, scoffing.

He narrows his eyes at her. "Do you have a problem with that?"

She lowers her chin, shaking her head as she scrapes the last bit of eggs off her plate. "No, sir."

He inclines a brow and then looks at me. Picking up his toast and a knife, he spreads jelly over it and then bites into it. As he does, he doesn't dare pull his line of sight away from mine.

He wants me to keep watching. This is his form of torture. Making me starve just because I was late for breakfast one fucking time. My belly growls loudly and embarrassment sweeps through me. He chuckles when he hears it.

"You heard that?" he asks the older woman.

She simply shakes her head and avoids his eyes, clearly disappointed in him.

"Oh, cheer up, mamá. This is how shit is handled. This is how you instill obedience. This," he says, wiping a thumb across his bottom lip, "is how you know they won't go against your word again. Francesca, what happens when someone is disobedient?"

"They are punished," she responds monotonously.

He watches me, studying my cleavage. I blink slowly, lowering my gaze a bit. I can't look away. As badly as I want to, I can't. He'll consider it a defiant gesture and I don't want to add to the days that I can't even get a crumb.

"You can drink your orange juice," he insists, pointing at it with his fork. "It's freshly squeezed. Shouldn't let that go to waste. Drink."

I grab it and take a small sip.

When I lower it, Francesca sighs. I'm not sure if she's with or against him. Either way, I know she won't step in or say anything.

And that's okay.

I don't need her to save me. I can save myself.

I may be hungry, but I was starving in that cell for six days and if I made it past that, I can get through this. I will not let his venomous ways fault my spirit.

I'll accept my punishment and then we'll move on from this mess and it will never happen again.

At 6 p.m. I'm not even allowed in the dining room.

Dinner is something Draco seems to take more seriously. He didn't want me here yesterday and he doesn't want me here today either.

The man with the white hair is at the door and he tells me to go back to my room before I can even walk in. I spot Draco sitting in his *throne*, twisting the silver skull ring on his pinky finger as he waits. His eyes are on me.

Stern.

Cold.

I turn without hesitation and go.

I go and I don't look back.

I take a shower, toss my hair up in a bun, and then climb into bed.

At 2:10 a.m. I hear those three footsteps again. The doorknob jiggles and I put my focus on it. It creaks open, but barely. A hand wraps around the edge of the door. It's a tan hand, a skull ring on the pinky finger.

I remember that ring.

Draco wore it during breakfast and dinner.

It's *him*.

Has he been the one tiptoeing past my door? I wait for him to come in and say something, but the door remains cracked. His hand is still wrapped around the edge, but in the blink of an eye it's gone.

The door shuts quietly and his footsteps drift down the hallway.

I listen until I can't hear them anymore.

I stare up at the canopy with tired eyes. My belly growls in agony while my heart skips a rapid beat.

Why in the hell is he doing this?

DAY NINE

At 7:50 a.m., I'm trudging down the stairs.

I walk to the french doors and see only Francesca and the older woman sitting at the table. Draco's place isn't even set, and I find utter relief in that.

They both look at me, but mainly Francesca. The older woman is knitting as she waits, her square glasses placed on the bridge of her nose.

"He's not going to be here for breakfast today," the older woman announces.

Oh, thank God.

She notices my relief as I walk forward and lowers her needles. "But you still can't eat. His orders."

"Seriously?" It feels like my stomach is eating my insides right now. It is in knots. I am so hungry. So thirsty.

"I'm so sorry," the older woman says. She drops her needles and I see the sympathy in her eyes. But just like everyone else, she knows she can't go against

Draco's word. Would he be so cruel as to harm his own mother just to prove a point?

Is he that callous?

Francesca doesn't look at me. She stares down at the plate in front of her. Pressing my lips, I turn around and walk out of the dining room. I look over my shoulder and Francesca is watching me go. Her expression is unreadable.

I don't know what the hell she's thinking.

She probably wants to kill me.

She thinks I'm the competition.

She's wrong. She can have that brute.

Instead of going to my bedroom, I walk towards the other kitchen, thinking maybe I can steal a bagel or a donut. It is vacant. It's already clean—no butlers or maids inside.

No food on the counters.

I sigh.

The door that leads to the beach is open. I walk out. But as I walk towards the sound of the ocean, I am caught up by the iron gates.

There is a lock box, but I don't know the code.

Defeat settles in. My fingers wrap around the thick, black bars, and I press my forehead between them, sighing again, hot tears burning my eyes.

I can see the beach from here and it is so beautiful…but then I see an old brown building not too far away from the shore and my heart sinks.

There are men standing outside of it, smoking cigarettes.

Ronaldo is still in there. I feel so sorry for him. I wonder how he's holding up. I wish I could go see him.

Francesca walks around freely, but she's succumbed to this lifestyle. I won't be. I'll take my chances.

I turn around, but as I do, Francesca is already standing by the door. Her eyes are hard on me, and she has a white towel in her hand. It's covering something.

A slight gasp fills the air when I see her.

Her face is solid, even as she walks towards me. For a split second, I think she's going to pull me aside and strangle me…but she doesn't.

"Here." She shoves the white towel into my hands. When it touches my skin,

I realize there is something warm inside of it. "He won't let you eat for another day. You're already too small. You'll faint before you make it. Eat that, but don't let anyone see you. Take it back to the bedroom. I'll bring you a water in a few."

She turns just as quickly as she appeared.

I watch her trot away in her tall black heels. She doesn't look back at me, and I don't blame her. I observe my surroundings before opening the white towel.

It's a biscuit with jelly and a half slice of ham on the side.

My mouth waters at the sight. I hear my poor belly cry.

I fold the hand towel back over and then cross my arms, making sure it's hidden beneath my palm.

I jog up the staircase and to my bedroom, shutting the door behind me. Rushing into the bathroom, I place the towel on the counter and carefully unfold it, as if I'm unveiling some sort of sacred treasure.

The biscuit is so soft that it's crumbled a bit, but it doesn't matter.

I will inhale every single buttery crumb.

I dig into it without hesitation. I don't care if she's poisoned it. Death already lurks here. At least I'll go out with some food in my stomach.

It takes me less than a minute to eat it.

When I look up into the mirror, my jaws are puffed, full of bread. I laugh at myself, planting my hands on the edge of the counter and chewing. I savor every bite, shutting my eyes and then swallowing it.

I eat the ham next and then I ball the hand towel up, stuffing it in the trash bin. I can't leave any evidence hanging out. It was great—and I'm grateful—but not nearly enough.

I walk back out of the bathroom, wiping the back of my arm over my mouth. As I do, there is a knock at the door. I stop in my tracks, staring at the jiggling doorknob.

"It's just me." Francesca's voice picks up from the other side and I rush for the door to unlock it. She surges past me, and I shut the door behind her.

As soon as I turn, she tosses the bottle of water my way. I crack it open and guzzle it down.

As I drink, she watches me.

PASSION & VENOM

I release a refreshing sigh and then put my attention on her. "Why are you helping me?"

"Because no one else will."

"I thought you didn't like me."

"I don't much," she assures me, folding her arms. "But it doesn't mean I don't understand what you're going through."

"He did this to you too?" I ask quietly, and she looks down, focusing on the tips of her heels.

"That...and other things. The other things were bad, yes, but not eating was the worst of them. I know how you feel. I know it's not fair. Just like you, I was only a few minutes late. He punished me for it. It's what he does. He punishes people in his own way for what he thinks is disobedience."

"But he should understand," I snap, walking forward. "I didn't have a clock. I didn't know what time it was at all."

"There are clocks in the kitchen, the bonus rooms, and in his room...but no one is allowed to go in there. You should have checked the kitchen. That's what he told me the day he finally let me eat. Four days," she stated.

"So after tomorrow he'll let me eat?"

"Maybe. He's different with everyone." Her face turns serious. "What did you do with the towel?"

"I threw it away."

She shakes her head. "Where?"

"The bathroom." She marches past me to the bathroom and I hear rustling. When she returns she has the towel in hand.

"You have to burn it. The people here are Draco's eyes and ears while he's away. They will snitch on you in a heartbeat for a quick, easy reward. Look," she sighs, "if you don't get on the same page as everyone else, you will suffer here. I was just like you—wanting to be strong. Trying to tough it out. Trying to stand up for myself and hoping it would gain me some respect, but I was wrong. And stupid. Draco doesn't give a shit about anyone else having respect but himself."

"He obviously cares for you," I murmur. "He lets you eat breakfast with him."

"And he wanted you to eat with us too. Doesn't mean that he cares. He's just being Draco. Confusing and twisted as fuck."

"So...what are you trying to say? That we have to be his *pets* in order to make it around here?"

She cocks her head. "No. We just have to do what we need to do to survive." She walks around me and grips the doorknob. "I know you're thinking about running away, but don't be foolish. He tells you that you can run, but Draco isn't that lenient. He'll let you run for a little while, but like a cheetah he'll catch you and drag you right back to where you belong...which is here. And he won't bring you back without getting a little blood on his hands. He won't trust you out there...and even if you got away, you wouldn't get far. Wherever we are—it's a bad city. If they see someone like you running free, they will fuck you like brutes, pass you around for money, and then gut you like a pig when they find you useless. Be smart." She holds out her wrists, showing me the old scars around them. "Or you'll wind up just like me."

She swings the door open and walks out. I listen to her go, her words replaying over and over again in my head. I know she's right, but I still won't cave that easily.

After tomorrow, I'll be able to eat again. Food is what I need. Fuel. I can't make a plan on an empty stomach and tired mind. I need rest and energy.

I should do what's best to survive around here, but Draco knew my father and he wasn't an enemy. That means he sees something in me. And to me that means I can probably get away with a lot more than anyone else around here can.

He's familiar to me. I remember seeing him before...a long, long time ago.

But the memory is so dim that not even the sun can bring it to light.

I slouch on the edge of the bed, staring down at my feet.

"It's day nine here," I murmur. "And I miss you so much, Toni. If you were alive, I know you would save me. I know you would kill him right in front of me if you had to...and I wouldn't even think differently of you. After what he's done to me—what he's done to *you*—I would take him down myself."

DAY TEN

My *alarm clock* goes off at 7:15 a.m.

My outfit for the day is already hung up on the wall.

I climb out of bed and go to the bathroom to pee. Afterwards, I start the shower, making sure to really scrub my hair and body.

I didn't hear the footsteps last night, and I'm glad. Draco didn't come around all last night, which means those were most likely his footsteps patrolling my bedroom and him peeking in at night.

After taking care of my hygienic needs, I brush my wavy hair and then get dressed in an orange and yellow dress. I slide into the sandals and then walk out of the bedroom.

There is a lot of commotion today.

I hear someone vacuuming one of the rooms. A man and a woman's voice is shouting in Spanish from downstairs. They both sound angry.

I step down slowly and when I make it to the bottom of the staircase, I look over to see Francesca and the white haired man standing in the den. She's pointing a finger, speaking rapidly.

He points towards the door and then points up.

She scoffs and then flips him off. She storms away from him, in my direction, and I collect myself, looking away rapidly, but I'm sure she saw me watching.

I know for sure she did when she says, "Let's go. We have two minutes." She continues her walk past me and I follow her.

I glance back at the white-haired man. He's frowning at us, his arms folded.

"What was that about?" I whisper.

"He's a fucking asshole."

"What do you mean? What happened?" I try and keep up with her but she's a fast walker. Her legs are much longer than mine.

"Draco knows," she says, and then winces.

"He knows what?"

"That I gave you the food…and water."

"What?" I gasp. "How?"

"Because Bain told him. That fucker I was just talking to."

"He saw us?" My voice comes out panicked and rushed.

"No…but one of the maids did and they told him." She glances over at me, and the look in her eyes isn't a good one. It's like she knows something is coming, she's just not sure how bad it will be.

"Francesca…shit, I'm so sorry."

"No. I'm sorry," she retorts. "I knew I shouldn't have listened to my heart. It always fucks me over in the end."

"I'll take the blame."

"We're both to blame and he knows it." She shakes her head and then walks faster to get to the dining hall.

As soon as the door is slung open, she walks right in, even as Draco sits in his chair with his dark glare fixed on us. His elbows rest on the arms of his chair, and I realize as I follow behind Francesca and take my chair that it isn't her he's watching.

It's *me*.

I glance at the clock. We have less than thirty seconds. At least we made it, but we shouldn't have cut it this close.

Draco's silence is deafening. As we sit here, waiting for the food to arrive, I feel suffocated. I'm not sure what to expect either, but with the way Francesca reacted, I know not to expect him to be lenient.

I just hope he doesn't try and starve me for another day. I don't care what happens to me as long as it isn't that.

The butlers come out with the breakfast. This time everything is set up on white plates, sort of buffet style. They place everything on the middle of the table and set it all up nicely.

There are croissants, chocolate filled pastries, waffles, sunny side up eggs, bowls of fruit, and pineapple juice.

"I hope you enjoy it, Jefe," one of the butler's says in Spanish as he backs away.

Draco nods, but his eyes don't pull away from me.

When the butlers are gone, I remain still. The older woman grabs some fruit and croissants, glancing at us several times.

Francesca doesn't dare move.

"Eat. Both of you," Draco commands.

Francesca doesn't hesitate to grab some food. I do.

I don't get the game he's playing. I expected him to punish me further, but at the same time if he's allowing me to eat, I won't resist.

I pick up a little bit of everything and as soon as I dig in, I can't help myself. I feel like a savage as I eat, but I try to do it diligently. I don't normally eat this fast, but it's been four days.

The pastries are hot and the fruit is so crispy and fresh.

It all combines into one beautiful breakfast and for a moment I forget that Francesca and I are under his radar.

"So you two have become good friends within the past twenty-four hours." Draco looks over at Francesca.

She rapidly shakes her head. "No, Jefe. We aren't friends."

"That's not what I heard." I stop chewing slowly when he watches me. "Bain tells me someone saw you give her food in a towel, and that you burnt that towel to make sure there wasn't any evidence later on."

Francesca stays quiet, lowering her line of sight.

"Is that true?" Draco demands, his voice growing irritated.

I chew wholly and respond for her. "Yes, it's true. But it's because I asked her to do it."

His chin tilts, those brown eyes trained on me. "And why the fuck would you do that when I made it clear you couldn't eat?"

"I was really hungry," I whisper.

He looks down at my nearly empty plate. "But I see you aren't hungry now."

"No, sir."

"And that's because I allowed you to eat. All you had to do was wait one more day, but instead you go behind my back and pull your sympathetic bullshit just to get a few forbidden bites."

I swallow thickly, my face turning bright red.

"And you fell for it, Francesca, didn't you? I guess I can't blame you. Look at her. With those big green eyes and her nice hair. That flawless skin and that plump ass she flaunts in those dresses."

Francesca doesn't say a word but I can tell she's uncomfortable with where this is going.

"She makes it easy to sympathize for her. I did the same damn thing when I took her out of those cells—when I took *you* out of those cells." He drops his fist on the table. "You knew better!" he barks at her and she flinches. "You fucking knew better." He shoves out of his chair and then walks behind her, planting his large hands on the armrests of her chair. His mouth is less than an inch away from her ear. "And because you knew better, I will make you beg for my forgiveness." His eyes flash over to mine. "I will make *both* of you beg."

He snatches his body away and Francesca flinches.

"Eat up and fucking enjoy it," he calls. "It's 8:12. Both of you better be in the galería in exactly two hours. Don't show and I will make the punishment worse." He's out of the dining room before we can even blink.

My gaze drops to my plate, and then rolls over to Francesca. She has her fork in hand, running it over the yolk of her eggs.

"You shouldn't have said that," she mutters.

"Why? I'd rather take the blame. You were being generous. You don't deserve to be punished for being kind."

"Draco isn't keen to kindness," his mom states. I look up at her and she releases a heavy sigh. "Eat as much as you can now. He may not let you eat again for a while after this."

"You tolerate his behavior?" I spit at her.

Her brows dip, and I can tell she's angry now. "He is my son. I will defend whatever he does."

"If it were you giving me that food, would he punish you for it?" I muse, narrowing my eyes.

"He wouldn't dare. My son has provided for me in ways no one else has. I know he may not be in a good, clean business but no one here is involved in clean business. He takes care of me and that's all I can ask for. What he does during his free time is not my business."

She bites into her pastry, glaring at me. Her eyes look just like Draco's, and the longer she stares, I become nervous. I don't want to get on her bad side. If Draco is to listen to anyone at all, it will be his very own mother.

I look at Francesca. She angrily pushes out of her chair, storming towards the door. She's gone before I know it.

I pick up my juice and drink some of it. I won't pass up the opportunity to eat. I will eat as much as I can, but I have to admit that I'm afraid of what's to come.

What does he have in mind?

What will he do?

What if he slices our throats one by one? What if he rapes us while making us watch?

Suddenly, my appetite is lost. I finish my juice and then push out of my chair, walking out of the dining hall and back up the stairs without looking back. I can feel Mrs. Molina watching.

As I walk up, I see the white haired man. Or Bain, as they call him.

He passes by me with a smirk on his lips, like he wanted this to happen.

Fucking asshole.

It's like he wants Draco to let me off his leash, just so he can do whatever he wants with me. He knows that once Draco is fed up with me, I'll be on my own. I won't be protected…and Bain will take full advantage of that.

Those two hours Draco granted us roll by way too quickly.

With each minute that ticks by on the alarm clock, I can feel my pulse accelerating. My heart is slamming in my chest when the final minute appears.

I haven't changed clothes.

I'm wearing the same thing.

I was too nervous to even bother.

I walk down the marble staircase and it's much quieter in the house now. I don't see any maids or butlers around. I don't even see any of his men. Did he want it this way?

The hallways are clear, the long corridor that leads the way to the art room vacant.

I take the next set of stairs gradually.

I can hear classical music playing from a distance.

He's in there.

I can sense him.

My feet drag towards the door. It's cracked open and I'm sure that's on purpose. When I open it and peek in, Draco is standing in front of a canvas that is covered in red, black, and yellow colors.

Francesca is already here, sitting on a stool in the corner.

Her eyes shift up to mine and she presses her lips. The look in her eyes is upsetting to bear witness to. She's just as nervous as I am, I know it.

"Shut the door." Draco's voice echoes across the large room.

I shut the door and he turns halfway, walking to the stereo system in the wall and turning the music down a notch. He looks over his shoulder at me, his hard eyes watching intently.

"Upstairs," he commands. "Both of you."

I look up, remembering the bed that's up there.

Oh my God. I was right. He *is* going to rape us.

Tears line my eyes as Francesca stands from her stool and walks towards the staircase. I remain absolutely still, watching as she makes her way up without so much as a glance back.

Draco comes in my direction, his footsteps heavy, and when he's right in front of my face, he grips the back of my arm and shoves me forward.

"Don't make me repeat myself."

I notice the first two buttons of his shirt are undone. His tan slacks sit low on his hips, his sleeves rolled up.

I drag my weight up the stairs and he follows closely behind me. I can smell his cologne. I can feel him on me. He's so close that the hairs on the back of my neck stand on end.

When I reach the top, Francesca is standing by the wall. Her face is bleak. She's ready to get this over with—whatever *this* is. She's obviously grown accustomed to his punishments by now.

"Take off your clothes."

My gaze flies up to meet his when his voice cuts through.

His expression remains even, one of his eyebrows cocked.

Francesca starts to undress, peeling off the straps of her purple tank top. Next, she unbuttons her jeans and then bends over to slide them down. She does it so casually that it makes me nauseous.

"Hurry up," he snaps at me.

Jolting, I reach up and pull the straps of my dress down. He walks behind me, examining my every move, his fingers meticulously rubbing his sharp jawline. When he makes his way back around, he's narrowed his gaze.

"It won't happen again," I plead, trembling. "I swear."

My body feels so cold and empty right now.

"Oh, I know it won't," he assures me, and his tone is so confident that it proves only one thing. He's going through with whatever he has planned and he's not backing down.

When my dress is around my ankles, I stand still.

He shakes his head. "Bras." He motions towards Francesca as he looks at me.

She unlatches her bra, and her full breasts bounce as she drops it. Her nipples are a light shade of brown, already pebbled and thick.

Draco doesn't bother looking over at her. She's completely naked now, and I'm surprised he doesn't give her at least a sideways glance.

My hands shake as I reach behind me.

"Do you need help?" Draco questions irritably.

I shake my head. I don't need help. I just don't want to do this.

He walks around me, bringing his hands up and pulling on the strap of my bra. He unhooks it and it snaps against my back, causing a light sting.

"There. Now take it off. Your panties too."

I'm on the verge of tears he walks around to face me again. I won't cry, though. He's had enough of my tears. When my bra and panties are gone, I start to cover my chest, but he grabs my wrist, nostrils flaring at the edges.

"You cover up, and I will make this a lot worse." His face is strict, that firm jaw pulsing again. I drop my hands slowly and he steps back. He points towards the bed that's set up against the wall. "Lie down on your back and keep your legs open."

My trembling body moves ahead. I sit first and then rest my back on the white comforter, staring up at the ceiling. The back of my head lands on the wide oak headboard.

"Francesca," he calls.

"Si, Jefe?"

"Come here."

I hear her feet shuffle as she walks towards him.

"Look at her now…like this," he rumbles. "Doesn't this make you want to help her even more?"

Francesca is quiet. I look up and she's looking away.

He grips her chin and forces her eyes on me. "Look. At. Her."

Her bottom lip quivers as she stares down at my legs. Her eyes are absent though. She's looking, but not absorbing like he is.

Draco releases her chin and then shoves her forward. "Since you don't want to answer me like a good girl, get on your fucking knees and face me." His tone is angry now.

She collapses on the bed, but pushes herself back up. She's on all fours now,

PASSION & VENOM

and she starts to rise, but he presses a hand on her back, forcing her to stay down.

"Actually," he smirks, "I change my mind. Don't get on your knees. Stay just like that."

She remains crouched at the end of the bed and he moves to her right, looking between the two of us.

"Since you want to give my shit away without permission, you're going to take it right back from her. Every bite she had that morning. Every taste. Every *lick* and *suck*—you'll take it all right back from her." His eyes flash with a wickedness that makes my insides twist uncomfortably.

Francesca looks up at me, unblinking.

"Move up and put your face between her legs."

She does at told without hesitation. When she's close, I start to recoil, but when I look at him, he grimaces, threatening me to remain still with his eyes alone.

Stepping forward, he rests one knee on the bed and looks me up and down. He stares at my pussy the most, but then he's looking at my C-cup breasts again.

Pressing the palm of his hand on the back of her head, he does just so until her mouth is hovering above my sex.

"And since you walked around seeking sympathy—begging with those big green eyes of yours, Gianna, well...how about you just keep begging then? You accepted what she gave you yesterday, and what I provided this morning, and you'll continue to do just that. Right now. Accept *everything* we have to offer."

His firm stomach presses on the outside of my knee as he leans in and looks down at Francesca. "Now eat her pussy and don't stop until she cums."

My stomach flips upside down. I look up at him incredulously, my heart pounding in my chest.

"What?!" I wheeze.

"Draco, I—" Francesca starts to speak but her sentence is short lived.

Annoyed with us both, he forces her mouth down and when her tongue glues to my clit, I gasp much sharper this time.

Francesca looks up at Draco, still pleading but not pulling away.

His nostrils flare, his hand delivering a rougher push. "Eat. Her," he snarls. "Be glad it isn't worse than this."

Francesca's eyes swoop up to mine and I squirm. They soften a touch as if she's apologizing in advance for what's to come. Then she catches me by total surprise.

Her soft, wet tongue presses down on my clit and she sucks on it. Heat shoots through my body, and I cry out again, my back arching.

"Please," I beg, looking up at Draco. But his face remains even. I'm begging, and that's exactly what he wants, but it won't be enough for now. He needs more. I can tell by the flames in his eyes—his lips that are smashed together. He's hardly holding onto restraint.

Francesca swirls her tongue in slow, torturous circles, the hotness of it overwhelming my entire body. I have never done anything with a woman and I never thought I would.

This forced act should infuriate me to no end and my body should be against this, but when she grips my thighs, moans between my legs, and then pushes them up until my feet are near the headboard, I realize I am in ultimate bliss right now.

After being tortured and punished. Abused and pushed over. After being dealt such bad hands, I finally feel like I'm being rewarded instead of neglected.

Francesca's tongue slides from my clit to the hole. She pulls one hand away from my leg and thrusts her fingers inside me, dragging her tongue back up to my swelling clit.

"Oh, God!" I scream, bucking.

"Feels good, huh?" Draco smirks down at me with heated eyes.

"Yes," I pant, raking my fingers through my hair. *Why did I just respond to him? I hate him!*

Draco grabs Francesca's hair, yanks on it, and then forces her face deeper into my pussy. She moans loudly, but her fingers don't stop thrusting and her tongue doesn't stop rolling.

No. In fact, she licks me faster.

It's almost like she's done this sort of thing before with a woman. She knows exactly where to place her fingers. How to stroke and rub with her soft, smooth tongue.

My body shakes wildly. I drop my legs and sit up halfway, looking down at her. Her big gray eyes hold mine, and then she sighs, doing what I never thought she would: indulging in my taste.

The sight of her there, between my legs, tasting me, almost *owning* me, is enough to tip me over the edge.

Draco still has his hands in her hair, forcing her head back and forth. And as I glance over, that's when I notice it. The large, solid bulge in his pants. It's extremely hard to miss.

I look up at him and he watches me with those hot brown eyes. He doesn't speak. He doesn't even react. But what he does next surprises me.

As if he can't resist the urge, he leans forward and his mouth comes crashing down on mine. His hot tongue slips through my lips, parting my mouth, and that's when I explode.

I moan loud and raggedly into his mouth, but he continues playing with my tongue, rolling his around mine as I release. He locks my face in one hand, using the other to make sure Francesca catches every single drop.

She glides her tongue over my tender, swollen clit more than once, and I quake under the pressure, grasping onto him, breathing deep and erratically.

He finally breaks the kiss, releasing my face and Francesca's hair.

She sits up a little with haste, wiping her mouth with the back of her arm. She's still between my legs, looking between Draco and me, wearing an unsatisfied frown.

I can feel him still watching me unravel, but I am too embarrassed to look at either of them for too long right now.

She just...ate me out and I enjoyed it way too much.

And that kiss.

My God, that kiss.

I hate him, I really do, but damn those lips.

Damn him for giving me this illicit pleasure.

He pulls away and walks to the corner to grab what looks like a paddle. It's made of solid wood, with a long handle and a thick board.

When he comes back, it takes me by total surprise when he grips the back of Francesca's neck, forces her body forward so her ass is showing, and then spanks her with it. His jaw clenches as he spanks her five times.

With each strike she's biting into her bottom lip, tears lining up at the rim of her eyes. He hits her hardest during the fifth strike and she yelps so loudly that I cringe for her.

Dropping the paddle, he grabs a handful of her hair and roughly yanks her away from me. She hisses through her teeth, but says nothing. Like a ragdoll, she takes it. She ends up on the edge of the bed and he finally lets go.

"Go get cleaned up," Draco orders, and I realize he's only talking to her, not me. She looks at him and then at me. Her lips are still pink, wet, and raw, as well as her ass.

She climbs off the bed, picks up her clothes, and then walks towards the stairs while rubbing her behind, but of course she looks back. She watches Draco, how he ogles me like a hawk.

The look in her narrowed gaze tells it all: Why hasn't he done the same to me too?

Hell, I hope he doesn't. It looked painful.

When she's gone, Draco steps closer to me.

"You want more of that?" he asks.

I shake my head rapidly. "No."

"You enjoyed it."

"I had no choice but to," I retort.

"Oh, you had a choice. We always have choices, you just chose the wiser one this time." His crooked grin really gets under my skin.

"Why would you make her do that?"

"That wouldn't be her first time eating pussy."

"You're a pig," I spit. "We aren't your fucking toys."

He frowns, taking the final step it takes to be pressed against me. He reaches down and grabs my forearm, yanking my hand up to grope the rock in his pants.

"Who do you think I'm hard for right now?" His voice comes out deep and husky.

"Her."

"You know damn well it isn't her. If it was, I would have told *you* to leave." He watches my reactions carefully. "I saw how you looked at my cock. I felt how you shuddered when I kissed you. You want to hate me, but I know you want my cock just as badly as I want your pussy, Gianna." He leans forward and his lips press on the bend of my neck.

My veins flood with fire, but I try to stay content.

"I'm leaking like a motherfucker after watching you cum all over her mouth like that."

I swallow hard.

He sits down on the edge of the bed, wrenching my legs apart. I whimper as he brings his hand between my thighs and runs a thick finger deep inside me. I helplessly sigh as he begins to play with me.

He watches me—how my head tips back and my mouth parts. I can't even believe I'm letting him do this to me. I can't believe I'm even feeling this way—wanting this after what he's done to me.

This man has ruined my entire life and yet I'm craving parts of him that shouldn't.

Bringing his hand up, he sticks his finger through my parted lips. "Suck."

I suck it away, tasting my deceit.

"I bet it's sweet," he murmurs. "Feels tight, too. So tight I may need to break you in."

He pulls back, releasing a sigh. "But the sad thing is disobedient little girls don't get a taste of my cock. You'll ache for me," he murmurs, gripping my thigh lightly. "And then you'll beg some more. And then you'll learn. You'll learn that obedience and submission gets you rewarded in so many ways—ways you could never imagine. But disobedience will leave you desperate and hungry...and you don't want that, *niñita*."

His face goes rock solid as he gradually pulls his finger out of my mouth and stands up. His cock is still hard, the bulge massive above me. With a swift shake of his head, he walks towards the stairs.

"Be at dinner on time tonight." He peers over his shoulder. "I think you've learned your lesson by now, haven't you?"

I nod.

He turns to face me with a frown. "I didn't hear you."

"Yes, I learned my lesson, sir."

A smirk plays on the edges of his lips. Walking down the steps, he says,

"That's a good niñita."

When he's down the stairs, I hear the bottoms of his shoes clicking as he walks to the door. As soon as I hear that door shut, relief swims through me. I gather my dress from the floor and put it on quickly.

I hate that my legs feel so wobbly and my body is so relaxed. I need those pent-up frustrations back.

I hate that he made her do that to me.

Now it will be awkward when I see her. Perhaps those were his intentions. He wanted us to distance ourselves. He didn't like that we were getting along…and I wonder why.

What's so bad about making a friend…or at least having someone with the same problems to talk to?

The last time I've felt this way down *there* was when Toni would take care of me. I can't believe myself. I'm so ashamed.

I feel like I've betrayed my husband by letting Draco touch me that way. Tears instantly blind me and I sink back down on the bed.

The tears are hot and heavy, and they don't hesitate to fall. I crouch forward and cup my face, swiping roughly at the unwanted tears, trying my hardest not to sniffle just in case he returns and hears me.

That wasn't supposed to happen.

When I got married to Toni, I made a sacred vow to him that I would never hurt, betray, or cheat on him. But I feel like I just have…even though he isn't here.

I don't understand Draco.

He knows I was married to the enemy, so why wouldn't he treat me as such?

He shouldn't trust me.

I would do dangerous things just to get out of here, including *murder*.

When I've pulled my shit together, I roughly swipe the tears away and then hurry towards the door.

I walk up the stairs to get to the corridor. I spot the white-haired man coming in my direction and I freeze. His strides continue, his sneer grating my nerves.

"Remind me to ask Francesca how your pussy tastes," he chuckles as he walks by. "Listening to you moan like that makes me want to fuck that juicy cunt even more now."

I hurry past but I feel him looking back at me. I don't bother. He's a filthy animal and I wish he would disappear already. He's an asshole and a snitch. He told on Francesca for helping me and he got nothing out of it? What was the point?

When I'm inside my bedroom, I lock the door and hurry for the bathroom. I take a long, hot shower, hoping to rid myself of any trace of Draco. I don't want to remember what just happened. I can't even imagine how Francesca feels—being forced to do that to another woman.

I can't imagine myself doing it. It's not something I'm accustomed to. I love cock, but I can't deny how amazing it felt to have her there between my legs.

Damn it.

Stop.

Don't think about it.

Just forget it ever happened.

DAY TEN
CONTINUED

There's a window in my bathroom that I didn't notice until now. I didn't notice it because it's a small, rectangular window that is high up on the wall, way above the toilet.

A toddler wouldn't even be able to fit his head through it.

I stand on the tank of the commode, my feet hanging off the edge. My fingers grip the windowsill and as I peer out, I see nothing but shimmering, turquoise water.

A never-ending, vast body of blue.

I look to the right and that's when I see the little brown shed they have Ronaldo in. There aren't any men outside of it today, which makes me question if Ronaldo's still alive.

I watch the brown shed for a long time, hoping to see someone walk in or come out, but there is no movement. The sun is setting behind it. I remember knowing when the sun was setting in there, from the small window in that cell.

I hated the sunset then because it meant nightfall was coming soon. There

PASSION & VENOM

were no lights in that cell. I could hardly see Ronaldo when it became dark—not unless the moon decided to burn bright.

Sighing, I step down from the commode. I plant my feet on top of the toilet seat and crouch a bit, but as I spin around, I spot a large body standing between the frames of the door. I clutch my chest, panting rapidly.

"What the hell?!" I blurt out.

My eyes meet heavy, brown ones, along with furrowed eyebrows.

"I put you in this room for a reason," Draco murmurs. "The windows can't be unlocked in here." He takes a slow step forward. "You can't run away. And even if you could, why would you want to?"

"I wasn't thinking about running away." Though it would be nice to escape.

"So what were you thinking about up there?" He gestures towards the window with a bob of his head.

I look away, unsure if I should ask. I don't think I should. He shouldn't know that Ronaldo and I were buddies in that cell. If he suspects it, he might break him even more. He'll make assumptions and I can't have that.

So I lie. "I was wondering if I could go to the beach sometime."

He cocks his head with thin lips. He doesn't say anything. He just stares at me.

The air is thick around us, and I notice how he looks from my cleavage to my legs.

"Get down," he orders. And I step down, folding my fingers in front of me. I run one finger over the diamond ring. "You think you deserve to go to the beach, niñita?" His fingers tilt my chin and I'm forced to meet his eyes.

I shrug. "I don't know."

He pulls his hand away. "I don't think so. You haven't been behaving very well."

"How can you expect me to behave after what you did to Toni?" I spit out.

He narrows his eyes and then points his gaze down to my hands. I don't realize that I'm twisting the ring around my finger, a nervous habit. With strict, chiseled features, he grabs my wrist and brings my hand up to view it.

Then, before I know it, his fingers are tugging at the ring, prying it off.

I yank away in an instant. "No! Stop! You can't take it!"

He stops tugging, his angry eyes meeting mine. "Are you telling *me* what to do?"

"No." I shake my head rapidly and my hair slaps my cheeks. "I'm not. I swear." My eyes burn. "It's all I have left of him. You can't take it. Please," I beg.

He holds onto my wrist, unblinking. His jaw pulses as he squeezes my wrist tighter, his fingers running over my skittering pulse.

"Fine." He steps back, dropping my arm. So much relief floods through me. I almost want to thank him, but in an instant my relief vanishes when he says, "Since you won't let me take it off, you take it off and hand it to me."

I stare up at him with an expression full of horror. Is he serious?

I don't even know why I wonder. I know he is. He doesn't joke around. He means this.

I hold my hand against my chest, as if I'm protecting a baby. "Why are you doing this?" My voice breaks.

"Because I fucking can. Now take it off." His voice is filled with so much rage that it confuses me to hear.

"I've never done anything to you, and whatever Toni did, I'm sorry about it, but you don't have to punish me for his mistakes!"

Draco chuckles, swiping a hand across his jaw. "You think I'm punishing you because of *him*?" His amusement washes away in an instant. "Trigger Toni is gone. My beef with him has been settled. But while you are under *my* roof, nothing of his will be here. Now. Take. It. *Off.*"

His thick eyebrows draw together as he sticks his hand out. His furious glare confuses the hell out of me. I don't get it. What have I done to deserve this?

I've been trying to fight my tears ever since the first night I cried in that cell. I fought them when he wouldn't let me eat, and even at night when he sneaks by my bedroom door. I fought them when he made Francesca do those things to me.

I have fought them every night, but I can't today. Today is just a really fucked up, shitty day.

This is all I have left of Toni, my husband, my life, and he's asking me to hand it over like it means nothing at all?

I know I can't fight him—I can't resist. If I resist, he'll punish me and I'm sure the consequence will be worse than not eating.

I twist the ring off and the hot tears that fall down my cheeks feel like lines of fire. My heart thunders in my chest, my entire body vibrating as I finally hand him the $25,000 ring, which meant so much more than money to me.

When it's in the palm of his hand, he clutches it, but doesn't pull his sight away from me. He takes one large step forward, getting so close to me that I can feel his body heat. He leans forward, and the stubble on his jaw grazes my cheek.

"You should know, niñita, that you are not his. He is gone and he's never coming back." He strokes the tears away from my left cheek. "Once you accept that, things will be so much easier for you around here. All you have to do is submit," he says, running a hand up my arm. My skin crawls in response. "Accept this fate. Do as you're told, please me, and things will go a lot smoother for you around here. Are you ready to accept this fate?"

I shake my head, grimacing up at him. "Fuck you," I hiss.

As soon as my words fill the already thick air, his hand comes up to my throat. He turns my body and forces me to step back so that my back hits the wall. He bares the top row of his teeth, his hand squeezing tight, but not so tight that I can't breathe.

We stare at one another with heated glares. He's looking from my eyes to my lips, and then down to my breasts. I can only focus on his evil face, my nostrils flaring.

It finally softens a touch and he releases me. I rub my neck and he releases a throaty chuckle.

"You'll come around, niñita. The smart ones always do, and from what I know about you, I know you are far from stupid." He raises a stern finger and points it at me. "You're angry right now, and I understand that. I can be an empathetic man, you see. But," he rasps, "the next time you speak to me like that, I won't be so merciful. Disrespect is another thing I don't admire, Gianna."

His hot gaze travels up and down the length of my body. Leaning forward, he tips my chin and presses his warm lips to the apple of my cheek. I hate the heat I feel sinking down to the pit of my belly.

"Make sure you dress nice tonight," he commands lightly, stroking my cheek. "I have something big planned for my new arrival after dinner." His new arrival, meaning me.

Pulling away, he turns his back to me and walks out. Before he disappears, I see him slide my wedding ring into his front pocket. Watching it sink in there, knowing it will be riding along with him as he walks around this house, makes my heart shrivel up in my chest. What will he do with it?

My heart is still slamming, my tears thicker and heavier.

I slide my back down the wall, squeezing handfuls of hair in my hands, unleashing all of the emotion and rage that I can longer contain. Taking my ring is the last straw. That was sacred and special to me.

I hate this place. I hate *him*!

Francesca was right. All he cares about is himself. All he cares about is feeding his ego.

I meant what I said to him. *Fuck him.* I won't accept this fate.

I won't be happy living with a man that isn't even happy with himself.

He needs to let me go. He'll get nothing out of me. Not willingly.

I stare into the mirror, eyes cold and distant, my arms at my sides.

My hair has been parted at the front and swoops over my right eye. I've pulled it back into a loose lower bun.

Normally, I would admire a gown like this—I would enjoy looking like this. I put on makeup because he wants me to look nice (and frankly, after he took my ring, I didn't think it was a bad idea to distract myself enough by looking pretty again.) My lips are glossed and I look great…but I don't feel like it at all.

The gown is made of embroidered sequined lace, with a boat neck and V-back. A ribbon sash is tied at my waist, the sleeves stopping mid-arm with a scalloped trim. It's the first black dress I saw in the closet when I was finally freed from the cells. My heels are a charcoal black, not too tall or short.

I give myself one more glance before walking out and looking at the alarm clock. I have ten minutes to make it down. I should get there early.

My numbness from earlier has consumed me.

I'm just going through the motions.

I can't think straight.

I keep thinking about Toni.

Flashbacks of my beloved husband are haunting me, almost as if he blames me for not standing up for myself and keeping my ring.

I blame myself too. I should have fought, but Daddy would always tell me that fighting over something that can be replaced is pointless. To Draco, it is just a ring, and my father would think the same of it.

I can cry all I want to, but it won't make a difference.

"Move ahead, Gia. Move ahead." Those were Daddy's words exactly. Even when I feel low, I have to keep going. Keep pushing. Don't stop or give up.

I won't.

And that's the only reason I'm going to this dinner.

The dining room is full of people when I enter.

I avoid frowning as I spot some of Draco's men standing in the corner. They aren't dressed as nicely as I am. Most of them are wearing brown or tan cargo pants with way too many pockets, black or gray T-shirts, and black gloves that don't cover their fingers.

His mom is sitting in her usual spot, wearing a brown gown, and Francesca is wearing a sheer white dress. Her hair is in loose, dark waves around her shoulders, her eyes down, focused on the empty plate in front of her.

She glances up and I force a smile.

She doesn't return it.

I feel the men looking at me, some of them grumbling to the next in Spanish, looking me up and down in my dress.

"Is that the bitch?" one of them with a slick black ponytail asks. He scans me thoroughly.

"That's her. Stupid cunt that got Pico bludgeoned by Jefe."

"What the fuck is he keeping her here for?"

"Probably same fucking reason he kept the bitch up there. To fuck her when he feels like it. She has a nice ass, though. I'd fuck the shit out of her myself. I don't blame him for keeping her too."

They all think I don't understand.

Fucking scumbags.

They both chortle but I ignore them, making my way towards the head of the table. I take my seat—two chairs down from Francesca—and place my hands in my lap.

I look around for Draco but he's nowhere to be found.

I peek at the clock. He has five minutes to arrive.

Those five minutes pass by rather quickly, and when he walks in from the kitchen, the butlers come out right behind him.

In his native tongue, he demands his men to sit and they all pull out chairs at the end of the table, a few seats away from us.

Draco pulls out his chair. He's changed clothes—a white button-down shirt with the sleeves rolled up and black dress pants. He's wearing the skull ring again, his black hair pushed back. He's gotten it cut. It's shorter on the sides and in the back, long and wavy at the top.

One loose strand has fallen onto his forehead and when he rakes it back and points his gaze on me, I feel my breath dwindle. The scary part is I don't know if it's in a good or a bad way.

Holding his hands out, he picks up his gaze and carries it across the table.

I didn't notice before that classical music is playing softly from the speakers.

His men notice him trying to get their attention and they stop talking immediately, putting all of their concentration on him.

"Thank you," he murmurs in Spanish, dropping his arms. "Tonight is special. Want to know why?" He flashes a wicked smile, but no one responds to his rhetorical question. "Because my guest is *finally* able to join me for dinner. She had to learn her lesson during these past few days, but I think she's starting to understand."

The men's deep laughter rides down the bare skin on my back.

"Francesca." Draco looks down at her and she perks up, looking him straight in the eye.

"Si, Jefe?"

"Trade seats with Gianna."

She freezes, her entire face going blank. She looks at him as if he's lost his mind. When he cocks a stern brow, she swallows hard and slides back in her chair. It makes a loud screeching noise across the floor.

I stare up at her as she watches her feet, waiting for me to rise as well.

PASSION & VENOM

"Gianna, up." Draco's deep voice fills the dining room.

I stand hesitantly, side-eyeing Francesca. She's completely avoiding my eyes now. I hope she doesn't think I asked for this, because I didn't. My only wish is to be as far away from that venomous monster as humanly possible.

I sit down in her seat, fidgeting when it's pushed forward by one of the butlers. The butler starts to push in Francesca's chair but she swats him away, bringing the chair in herself.

"How does that feel?" Draco coos to me.

"Fine."

"That's a good niñita." He takes his seat, and then cues the butlers. As soon as they get the order, three men with rolling carts walk out of the kitchen and start to place plates in front of us.

They aren't covered this time. I get an eyeful of the grilled asparagus, rice, baked salmon, and on the side are warm tortillas. The men at the end of the table rub their hands together, ready to devour their meals. Some of them already have their forks in hand.

A butler places a bowl of salad in between Draco, his mother, and me. Another at the end where the men are. I'm sure they won't even eat it.

Once the red wine is poured, we are encouraged to eat by the boss himself. As I eat, I can feel him watching me. His gaze is hot and heavy.

He's eating slowly. I avoid him at all costs.

I hate him for what he did earlier.

If I'd had the option to not show up for this dinner I wouldn't have.

"Do you know why I let my men eat dinner with me?" Draco asks quietly, leaning closer to me.

I stare down at my fish. "No, I don't know." *And I don't care.*

"Because they deserve it."

"How? By killing husbands?"

I finally meet his eyes and they are amused. "That's a great benefit," he says. "But not the only reason why. These men here—" he points at them with his fork "—they will do whatever I ask of them. They respect me, they handle my dirty work when need be, they keep the money rolling in, and in return they are rewarded. I don't mind taking care of anyone as long as they are doing their best to take care of me. Now, if one of them gets stupid and does what Pico did...well, you saw what happened. Idiots like him rot in cages until they can prove their worth again."

I swallow the hunk of tortilla I just bit off. "Is that where he is now? In that dungeon?"

"Yes."

I shouldn't be asking after what that son-of-a-bitch did to me... but... "When will he be out?"

Draco sits back in his chair, picking up a tortilla and grabbing a handful of rice with it. "I don't know. Whenever I see fit, I presume."

I look away, taking a bite of the fish.

"Francesca," Draco calls, and she brings her head up to look at him. "How is your dinner tonight?"

"It's great, Jefe." Her voice is deflated—lifeless, emotionless.

I side-eye her again.

"That's good."

Draco sips his wine and then stands up rapidly, clanking his glass with the edge of his fork. The men at the end of the table stop chatting to look at him.

I didn't even notice before that Patanza is down there with him. For some reason she blends in tonight with her hair tied behind her back, the cap on her head, and her baggy black T-shirt on.

Bain is sitting at the end of the table now. His eyes are on me, intense and desperate.

I pull my gaze away, doing my best not to flip him off. *Pig.*

"That's better." Draco motions for Bain to come up and he stands, walking past my chair and meeting up to the boss. Draco murmurs something to him in Spanish that I can't quite hear, and when Bain takes off, he begins to speak. "As you all can see, my new arrival is quite beautiful."

They all drop their gazes to me, and those savage guises arrive again. God, they are pigs. All of them.

"She's so beautiful you want a taste, right?"

"Fuck yeah!" one of them shouts with a mouth full of food.

Draco's smile evaporates immediately. "Well, you can get that thought out of your fucking minds right now. From this moment on, she will not be talked to and she will *definitely* not be touched. If I find out that any of you touched her in anyway, I will be sure to break your fucking hands off and stuff every single one of your grubby fingers down your fucking throats." The men are dead silent as they stare at him. "Is that fucking clear?" Draco barks.

"Sí, Jefe!" they all say at once.

"Good."

Bain comes back and when he meets up to the table I notice he has a black case in hand. He places it down on the table and then pops it open, revealing a red type of gun.

It's not the sort of gun that shoots bullets. This gun has a needle at the end of it.

"So now that we know that, it clearly means she is here to stay."

What?!

The blood feels like it's draining from my body as he picks it up. The meal I'm trying to digest seems to build right back up. I feel sick as he walks around his chair and demands me to stand up.

"Draco," I plead.

"Stand, Gianna. Now."

Bain pulls my chair out, leaving me no choice but to make a move. I stand on weak, wobbly legs, watching the gun with the needle. He inserts something very tiny into it and then steps forward.

"Turn around, niñita."

"W-what is that?" My voice trembles.

"This, Gianna," he breathes, resting a hand on my shoulder to spin me around. "Is so you can't run away. You are here to stay, and if you try, I will easily find you."

"What is it?" I ask again, feebler this time.

"A tracker. Hold still." He grips my shoulder and pulls a few loose strands of my hair away. After that, he slides the back of my dress over. Rubbing my shoulder, he murmurs, "It will sting just a bit, but don't worry. You've been through much worse."

The sharp end of the needle presses into the soft flesh right beneath my armpit. It sinks in and I hiss through my teeth, but I can hardly feel it.

I only hiss because now I really know…there is no way out of here.

Francesca was right, and as I look at her, I realize she didn't tell me this on purpose. He's done this to her too. He's made a tool out of her just to demonstrate his control—his power—but now it has switched to me.

"Why are you doing this?" I ask when he spins me back around. I rub the area, scratch it, but I can't even feel it. "How deep did you put it in there?"

"Deep enough that you can't cut it out without hitting something that will keep you alive."

"You are a fucking pig," I snap at him.

His face doesn't change. "I've been called worse. Now, sit the fuck down before you piss me off again."

I hold his gaze, on the verge of tears. He doesn't dare blink—not even a twitch. He simply stares back, and I know if I don't sit, he'll make an example out of me right here in this dining room. Right in front of his men.

I step away and sit, yanking my chair forward and staring down at my half-eaten food. My blood feels like it's broiling, my head like it's about to explode. My heart is thundering in my chest, and my palms are sweaty now.

I'm trying to hold in all of my rage—all of my emotion—but it's nearly impossible. He's a jackass. I have officially been trapped in hell, and Draco is the devil himself.

Draco puts the gun back in the case and sends Bain off with it.

It burns where he inserted the needle.

I have the urge to scratch at it, but I don't. I don't need any more attention being put on me.

"Let's finish eating," Draco insists, sitting back down and shooting his eyebrows up as he looks at his mother.

She studies her son, and it's like she questions how he became this way.

Her stare is blank, her eyes so lost and confused.

This poor woman.

She's raised a monster and she probably didn't even realize it until it was too late.

As everyone eats, I watch Draco closely as he talks to his mother about his plans tomorrow. He's so sure of himself that it pisses me off. His hair tumbles onto his forehead again, and I want to slice it off with the knife he's holding.

When he turns his head and meets my eyes, I realize I've been staring at him for too long. He points down at my plate. "Eat your food, Gianna. I wouldn't want you to go without again." He smirks.

When I pick up the fork, I squeeze it in my hands until I feel the edge of it pushing into my skin.

I feel the sting, but it doesn't hurt me as much as before. I look down at my lonely ring finger, the tan line there. My vision becomes blurry the longer I look at it.

But I eat, and pretend there's nothing wrong.

After dinner is over, the men are leaving the dining room to make way for the brown shed. I assume it's their hangout spot—where they smoke and boast while picking on Ronaldo.

Draco stands from his chair and leaves, glancing back once at me before stepping out.

Francesca rushes out as well and I see her run down the hallway after him.

All that's left in the dining room is his mother and me.

I'm finishing my wine, knowing damn well that I need it in order to relax and hopefully get a good night's rest. His mom has finished eating, but her attention is on me and it's making me feel out of place.

I finish off my wine and then stand, deciding to leave immediately. As I push my chair in, she calls after me.

"Wait…" She stands up slowly, and her gray hair sways as she comes in my direction. When she's less than a step away, she grips my shoulders and looks me dead in the eyes. "I wanted to wait until he was gone to say this. Listen to me closely." Her eyes are just as brown as his, but much gentler.

"Give yourself to him if you want to survive. It is that simple. Don't be stubborn. All he will do is knock that stubbornness out of you and then get rid of you once he feels like he's won." Her head shakes as she sighs. "My son can be hard to handle and even harder to seek compassion with, but he is that way for a reason. He may seem cold, but if someone can dig deeper, touch his soul, maybe...well, maybe he will change."

"Change?" I spit. "How can he *ever* change? He killed my husband. He took my wedding ring and it was all I had left." I yank away from her and her eyes spread wide. "I can't forgive him. Your son? He's a monster and you know it. He doesn't have any compassion. He's heartless and cruel and there is no changing someone like him."

"That's what you think, but you don't know him." She waves a hand. "He admires you a lot more than you think. He has been talking to me about you. And about your father."

I narrow my eyes and pause before speaking again. "You knew my father?"

"Sí...I knew him well enough. Your mother too. He was a good man, and that man is the only reason you are alive right now. So do as I say. Give yourself to him—all of you—and don't hold back. You want to get on his good side, you do as he says. You please and obey him. I would hate to see something happen to Lion's only child. I'm sure he raised you to be smarter than this—what you're doing now."

Lion? How does she know that name? That name was sacred for Dad. A secret name only people that were close to him knew and understood.

I look at her...speechless.

I don't blink.

I can hardly breathe.

She knew my parents, which means Draco knew them too. But if that were the case, why would he have his men kill Toni? Toni was close to Daddy too. Daddy trusted Toni.

"Survival is key here. Maybe, if you do right by him, he will do right by you and he will let you go. He'll know you aren't happy sooner or later. My son has a heart in there somewhere. He tries to cover it up with his demands and his punishments, but the heart is there. Francesca has tried to win him over, but it didn't work out for her because he doesn't care about her...but I think that you have a fighting chance. You have potential. You are beautiful and unique and unlike Francesca, you aren't *afraid* of him."

"No," I say boldly. "I'm not."

"Then you are already one step ahead. Think of it this way: your obedience could mean your freedom." She turns her back to me after that, leaving her words in the air.

When she's long gone, I stand still, my eyes trained on the floor.

The sad thing is, she's right. And I know it, but my pride is too damn thick for me to see through it right now.

If I don't drop this pride—if I don't at least try—I won't win.

He knows it. I know it. Everyone knows it.

I walk out of the dining room and make way for the stairs. When I'm inside my bedroom, I unzip the dress and step out of it. I walk to the closet and take down a nightgown.

But it's as I brush my teeth that I finally know what I need to do.

What I should have done all along.

The signs have been there.

The way he tiptoes past my bedroom late at night.

Making Francesca eat me out in his art gallery for his pleasure.

Kissing me so deeply he could feel my orgasm riding through his body.

Giving me her seat at dinner.

Tracking me so I can't escape or leave unless he wants me to.

Punishing me severely when I've done wrong. Rewarding me handsomely when I've finally done right.

In order to receive the ultimate reward—my freedom—I must do what everyone has been telling me to do. I have to do something I know I will hate.

I must submit to Draco Molina.

DAY ELEVEN

Sunlight has swept across my bedroom.

My curtains are drawn wide open, revealing the shimmering, turquoise water.

Sitting up with haste, I search the bedroom, wondering who in the hell has been here.

Everything looks the same. No one out of the ordinary is waiting for me to wake up.

But there is something here that wasn't last night.

Pushing out of bed, I tiptoe towards the black vanity. My mouth parts as I get close to the flowers in the vase. I've never seen flowers this dark before.

They are a blood-red color with a splash of brown and a hint of lavender. I touch the velvety petals, speculating where they've come from.

But then I notice the envelope beneath the opaque black vase.

I pick up the flowers and snatch up the envelope. On it are the words *Open*

PASSION & VENOM

Me in jagged, manly print. I look around the bedroom once more before opening the envelope.

There is a folded sheet of paper inside of it.

I open it and read it.

They are called chocolate cosmos. They are rare. Unique. Sweet smelling. They bloom when it is hottest here. You wanted a day at the beach, you can go after breakfast. Make sure you dress accordingly and don't be late.

-Draco

His signature is bold and just as jagged as the words on the envelope. I toss the paper on the vanity and then lean in to smell the flowers.

They smell like vanilla. It's a pleasant scent. Strong. Sweet, just like he said.

They've already been placed in water. I wonder how long they'll last.

I'm wary about them, though. What if there's a camera or something hiding between the stems? I sift through them, making sure nothing seems out of the ordinary.

Everything looks fine…but looks can be very deceiving in this place.

I'm surprised he's giving me the day to go to the beach. I get a giddy feeling just thinking about it. I'll be out of the house. Bathing in the sun. Maybe there's a way out. Maybe I can swim away to another place.

Maybe someone will find me and take me to the cops.

I can't miss out on this opportunity. I check the alarm clock. I have an hour to get dressed. I make way for the closet, searching through the clothes until I come across the untouched bathing suits hanging in the back with the price tags still attached to them. They are all nice, but one of them stands out the most to me.

It stands out because it looks like the bathing suit I bought for my and Toni's honeymoon.

It's all white, with a gold ring holding the fabric together. It's a two-piece bikini. It's simple, but it's perfect...and I hate it.

Our honeymoon was going to be amazing. I could picture it. Our bungalow was right on the beach. We'd wake up to water that is much clearer than the water here and we'd make love when we awoke in the mornings and then fuck like wild animals at night after getting drunk.

I had it all planned out.

But just like that, it all vanished right before my very eyes.

I stand in front of the mirror with watery eyes, staring at the bathing suit. It hangs limp in my hands, but I have to wear it. I'll pretend he's with me. I'll make it a good beach trip.

I wonder why Draco is rewarding me. Did I do something good? He put that tracker in me and I protested. Is he trying to worm his way in?

I hope he doesn't think it's working. I'll take things and use them to my advantage, but I don't owe him shit. If anything, he owes me.

It doesn't matter what he does, he will never be able to pay off the debt of a slaughtered husband on my wedding day. No price is high enough to compensate for the loss of love.

As I get dressed, I remember what his mom was saying about giving myself to him. I want out of here, and that means he has to trust me, even if I don't trust him myself.

That means I should worm my way in deep and do whatever it takes to own that man.

And that's exactly what I'll do.

I'll make him crave me.

I'll make him soft for me.

And as soon as he feels comfortable, I will seek my revenge.

If I play by my rules, I will be out of here before I know it.

Like Ronaldo said, I have a pussy. It's time for me to use it.

During breakfast, I feel Mrs. Molina watching me. She doesn't say anything, but she is looking. At first, I didn't mind the idea of going to the beach with her. She seems the most lenient of everyone I've met, plus she knew my father.

And if my father knew of the Molinas that means she may have some knowledge. But her odd looks and words from yesterday are playing a match of ping-pong in my mind. Why is she so concerned about what happens to me?

After I finish my sausage and egg tostado, I drink the rest of my mimosa and then stand up, picking up the towel from the back of my chair.

"Do you know the code to the gates?" I ask both Mrs. Molina and Francesca.

"No," Francesca responds without looking up.

"Yes." Mrs. Molina sluggishly pushes out of her chair. "But I am not allowed to tell you the numbers." She walks around the table, meeting up to me. "Come on. Let's go." She displays a gentle smile, walking past me to get to the french doors.

I start to follow after her, but Francesca reaches up rapidly to grab my wrist.

"Is he letting you swim?" she whispers, staring me right in the eyes.

"He said I could go to the beach."

"Why?" she hisses angrily.

I pull my arm away and shrug. "I don't know. He left a note in my room. I mentioned that I wanted to go yesterday."

She bats her eyelashes wildly and then drops her hands, staring down at the table.

I look around for listening ears and prying eyes before focusing on her again. "Can't you come with us?" I whisper in Spanish.

She shakes her head, her thick curls flopping. "No. And I won't ask. He hasn't spoken to me personally since he found out I helped you—besides the dinner last night, but that doesn't count. He was just putting on a show for you."

I frown. "For me?"

"Yes, you," she snaps, glaring up at me. "He's giving you way more freedom than I've ever gotten. He hardly punishes you. I've been here for three years. I've done everything he's asked of me, but he's never let me go out past the pool."

I look away, focusing on the floor. "I—I didn't know."

"Of course you didn't." She shoves back in her chair, and the legs scrape the floor. "Like he said, a pretty girl like you is hard to say no to. A pretty girl like you is obviously hard to punish too." She narrows her eyes, scanning me in my white

T-shirt and beach shorts. "I never should have fucking helped you. Ever since he saw you naked, he hasn't been able to keep his eyes off of you."

She turns around and storms through the kitchen. I watch her go, baffled by her harshness.

"Ignore her," Mrs. Molina says when Francesca's long gone. "She is simply in love with a man that will never be in love with her. Knowing that will always tear her up inside."

I turn around to meet Mrs. Molina's brown gaze. Wrinkles form around them. Waving a hand and gesturing for me to come her way, she says, "Let's go, before my son shows up and changes his mind."

"Right." I follow after her, leaving the dining room but not without one glance back. Francesca doesn't come back, but I feel awful. Guilty. I know she's right. I've noticed it too. She was just being nice to me that morning. I took the breakfast that day. I should have refused it. Maybe Bain never would have told on her.

I could tell from the moment I met her that she loves Draco. She loves him immensely, and he treats her like some caged dog, tossing her the scraps, punishing her over the smallest things.

He is attracted to me, that is apparent. Ever since he kissed me the day he forced her onto me and told me that he wanted me, I knew it. He said it out loud so there is no denying it.

He's doing all of this stuff—putting a tracker inside me, sending me flowers, and letting me go to the beach—but he knows damn well that I don't deserve his attention.

He knows damn well that if anyone deserves his rewards, it's Francesca. She is dedicated to him and she still has a heart.

And what he fails to realize is that my heart doesn't, and will never, beat for him.

It still belongs to Toni.

He can have my body, but he won't own my broken heart.

I rub the suntan lotion on my arms and legs as Mrs. Molina spreads her towel out. Her gray hair dances with the strong breeze. She gave me a pair of sunglasses and I'm rocking the hell out of them right now.

"It's a beautiful morning," she says, crouching down and then sitting. She bends her legs and looks towards the ocean. She has a pink straw hat on that matches her bathing suit. "I have to tell you, I think Draco is being very unfair with you."

I look over at her quickly. "Why do you say that?"

She shrugs. "Considering how close I was to your family. Your mom and dad especially." Her accent is thick as she forms a faint smile. Her voice is actually quite soothing.

"You were close to them?"

"Well, I wouldn't say we were best friends or anything, but yes. I talked with them and visited every time I came to the U.S. I haven't been there in years, though." She looks sideways. "I was very upset when I heard about your mom's diagnosis and then your father's death."

"You mean his murder." I raise an eyebrow, glad she can't see my angry eyes.

"Yes," she murmurs. "His murder. I hope they figure out who it was."

I sigh, looking forward. "If they haven't by now, I doubt they ever will. The cops were relieved he was gone. It meant he couldn't keep running deals in their area—that they knew of anyway. Whoever got to my father was smart about it."

I huff a laugh and she looks over at me. "What are you laughing about?" she inquires.

"I was just thinking…about something my husband Toni did." I swallow the lump in my throat. "He was so furious about the news. He looked up to my dad. My dad was pretty much his mentor. He brought him in, took him under his wing. He showed him the ropes. When it happened, Toni was in Washington handling some business. He was so angry—so hurt. He cried for hours behind closed doors with me when he came back. We…cried together." I smash my lips, hoping it will hurt enough to rid me of my unwanted tears. "He loved Daddy. Probably more than me," I laugh.

"I bet he did. Your dad was very loveable and charismatic. Your mom—I remember her being head over heels for that man. Their marriage…I would never admit this to them, but I envied it. I wished me and Mr. Molina were as close as they were, but he worked so much and then…poof. He was gone. Just like that."

She forces a smile, as if it doesn't cause her any pain just thinking about it, but I know it does. I know because I lost my husband too, and I didn't even get to spend enough time with him to grow a family or add years under our marriage belt.

I wonder what our first child would have been. Toni wanted a boy. I so badly wanted a girl. A mini-me. I'm not sure why. I guess seeing pink clothes and rosy cheeks was more appealing to me.

Now…well, I'd never raise a child in this sort of environment. Not unless I can get away. But even so, there is no one else I want to have a child with. Toni was the man I imagined as the father of my children. He was great with kids—wonderful, in fact. I couldn't wait to see how he'd take care of ours.

Anger blinds me and I push up to a stand, pulling my T-shirt off and then walking towards the ocean. "I'm going to test the waters," I say to Mrs. Molina without looking at her.

I can feel her watching me, but right now I have to remember that even though she is sweet, she is still Draco's mother. She is related to him and I have no doubt that she will tell him anything I said if he asks.

Her son called the hit on my husband. He still has my ring. I hate him, probably more so than she loves him. Yes, it's that deep for me.

I can't reveal too much. She'll snitch on me in a heartbeat.

I have to remain distant.

I feel her eyes on me as the cool blue water runs over my bare feet. I stare down at my splotchy toenails. The room I'm in has everything a woman needs. Nail polish, nail polish remover, pads, tampons, extra tissue, and a closet full of clothes.

I wonder if Francesca set all that up, or if Draco is so fucking sadistic that he keeps that specific room stocked for captors like me.

I can't think about it too much. When I think about how gracious I should be that he's even letting me wash and take care of myself, I want to hurl. But the ball in my stomach is so tight.

I've unleashed every emotion I've had.

I can't even cry anymore. I don't cry at night, but I wish I could.

It's like I've been drained of all emotions. I don't even understand myself anymore. What the hell am I doing? Why am I not trying to run away? Why

PASSION & VENOM

haven't I fucked the boss to get out of this place yet?

My brain is telling me to be wise, to use my body if it means escape but...I'm afraid. I can't.

Because when I think about doing something with it with someone else, I think about Toni, and how he'd feel so betrayed if he were still alive.

I think about how I should be honoring him by staying away from the man that had him killed.

I know he's watching...and he isn't pleased.

But Toni doesn't understand. In order for me to get out and truly mourn his loss, I have to dirty myself up a little. I can't pretend I'm not wanted.

"You know, Draco was really close to your dad too." Mrs. Molina pops up beside me and I gasp, clutching the heart of my chest.

"Ohmygosh!" My words come out rushed.

She laughs, holding her hands up innocently. "I didn't mean to scare you. I'm sorry!"

I wave a dismissive hand, laughing. "It's okay. I didn't hear you come up. I'm really jumpy lately."

"I guess I can understand that. Being in a place you don't want to be—not knowing what will come next." Her wrinkled lips twist.

"Yeah." I tuck a loose strand of hair behind my ear. "How was Draco close?"

"Ah—well, every summer, he would come with us to the U.S. His father wanted him to learn a few things about the business. He wanted Draco to follow in his footsteps. I was against it, but that bullheaded man never listened to me." She drops her head and look towards the ocean. "You two met once. He was sixteen, which made you about ten years old, maybe? You were young, but we were at a shooting range. You were doing homework while your dad and my husband were doing target practice. I was there, but we arrived late. I remember it so well because it was the first time I saw my son stare at a girl. He watched you like a hawk through the window. You had your headphones on to block the noise out, and as you wrote, he watched every so often. He kept saying he wanted to join the men, but I knew he just wanted to get a closer look at you." She smiles, as if she's so proud of what he did. "When your father charmed me into letting him go out on the range, you dropped your pencil while you were trying to erase something. It rolled near his foot so Draco picked it up. It was sweet to watch. He handed it to you without a word. He kept staring at you but you were so oblivious. You were young, so flirting probably wasn't a big deal to you." She titters. "He was…nicer back then. Somewhat innocent. I never wanted him to change his ways. Back then, he was still my young, loving Draco."

"So what happened to him? Why is he so cold now?" I ask softly.

"Muerte," she murmurs. "Death can make any person cold. Distant. Heartless. Especially if the death hits you hard." She drops her head, watching the waves ripple in. "His dad was important to him. My husband loved his son so much, and Draco knew it. I don't think it would have hit him as hard if he were away when it happened, but Draco was there with him and he witnessed the entire thing. I wasn't. I was here. But even being in here, I felt like something was wrong. I just had a bad feeling that day." Her head shook roughly. "Something wasn't right. When my son returned home…I couldn't even recognize his eyes. They were empty. Lifeless. I tried to hug him but he shoved me away. He didn't talk about it with me—still hasn't much to this day. If I mention his father too much, he starts to get angry."

"He saw his father die?" I whisper, my eyebrows pulling together.

She bobs her head. "Firsthand. One bullet to *la cabeza* was all it took. Draco believes it was a setup. He still has people looking into it. He thinks the person is still out there."

"Wow," I breathe. I guess that explains some of it…but not all. "I'm sorry," I utter.

She waves a hand at me. "Don't be. It is already done. I won't say I am at peace with it, but being married to a man like him, I knew what I was in for. It was a risk loving that man…but I don't regret it. He made me happy, even if for a little while." Her lips stretch wide to smile, and it's genuine. She steps back and then turns to pick up the white bucket beside her towel

"Normally when I come out here, I look for shells." She comes back with the bucket, showing me three of them. One is creamy looking, with a pink hue. Another has a blue tint. The last one is solid white, but it's spotless.

"They're beautiful," I tell her.

PASSION & VENOM

"Mmm-hmm. I need to look for more." She drops her arm. "I know you want to enjoy your time out here while you have it, so let's bask in this sun for a while. Enjoy this. Once I've gotten enough sun, I'll start doing some digging around to see what I can find."

I nod, grinning as I turn around. "Sounds lovely."

The sun has dropped since I've been out here.

I want to say it's been at least four hours, and I am perfectly content with that. I don't want this day to end.

I roll onto my back, the sun smothering my face and body. It feels nice and warm on my skin. I could soak in it all day.

I hear footsteps and look to my right. A shadow eclipses over me moments later, blocking the burning rays.

I look up, tilting my sunglasses down. I already know who it is before even making eye contact. I can smell his cologne.

Draco stands tall, his face smooth and clear of expression. His eyes are focused on my breasts. Slowly, his gaze travels down the length of my body—my hips as well as my oiled legs.

"Are you enjoying your time out here?"

I look down, noticing he's barefoot. "Yes," I murmur.

"Good. I'm glad." He looks towards the water and steps back. "Did you get my gift this morning?"

"Yes."

"What do you think of them?"

"They're...*beautiful*." I cringe when I admit it.

"I think so too. I have a whole garden of them. Maybe I'll show you sometime soon...if you behave." He flashes a crooked smile, bringing his head back up to search the area. "Where is my mother?"

"She went to search for shells. She has a collection of them already."

"Ah." He nods. "She does. A beautiful one too. You can find the best of anything here."

I pause before asking the next question, sinking my fingers into the hot sand. "Where…are we exactly?"

His eyes bolt on me and a smirk spreads across his lips. "Now, why should I tell you?"

"I'm just curious."

He looks me over thoroughly before turning his head and watching the waves crash in. The wind bristles by, pushing the loose strands of my hair away from my shoulders.

I know he's not going to answer that question so I take a different route. "How long are you going to punish Francesca?"

He immediately turns to look down at me, and fear blooms in my belly when his nostrils flare. "However long I please, niñita. She knew the rules."

"So did I," I state boldly.

"So, what are you saying? That I should scratch this whole thing and treat you like her?"

"No, that's not what I'm saying. I just…" I watch him tilt his head, ready for me to spit it out. "Never mind," I mutter, dropping my line of sight to my lap.

Draco lowers to a squat and then reaches forward to pick my head back up. When our eyes are glued, he drags in a breath before exhaling.

"You test my patience, Gianna. You question my ways. What you should do is worry about yourself while you're in my good graces. Don't worry about Francesca. She's a big girl. She can handle herself."

I nod. "Okay."

"Good, niñita." He releases me and stands up straight. "Since I've given you this reward, I expect to see you in the galería after dinner." I start to ask a question but he holds up a finger to stop me. My mouth clamps shut. "Don't ask questions. Just be there. Do you understand?"

"Yes, Draco."

His eyes spark when his name rolls off my tongue. He holds my eyes longer than intended, his head cocking again. His mouth twitches to form words, but as expected, he says nothing.

He simply turns around and walks towards his undeserved mansion. I watch him go before turning back around and staring ahead at the ocean. It seems to stretch so far, an endless supply of water.

While no one is here, I could try and swim it, but I don't think I'd make it very far. I'd end up getting tired arms and collecting lungs full of fluid before being found alive. The idea of it is scary, but at least if I'm dead in the ocean, he won't be able to find my body.

It would be deep in the abyss, sinking lower and lower, never to be found again…or floating.

I stand up and collect my things. As I fold my towel, my eyes venture over to the left and I see something flashing.

I blink, zeroing in whatever it may be.

It twinkles beneath the sun, fierce and bold. I step aside and spot a car. It's silver, but I'm not sure what make or model it is. I look around. No one is here.

Not his mom.

Not even him.

He's most likely rinsing the sand off his toes right now.

My heart thuds.

The first thing that comes to mind is one word…

FREEDOM.

No one is watching. I am unguarded.

Go, go, go!

I have to make my move *now*.

Run. Now!

I scurry across the beach without a second thought. There is a wrought iron gate when I make it across. I examine my surroundings. The windows are clear. His mom is still on the hunt.

Gripping the bars, I stick my foot on one of the bars and then climb up. When my hand wraps around the top of the gate, I swing my leg over, doing my best to avoid the sharp points.

My heart thunders heavily as I drop both legs on the bars on the opposite side. I can't believe I'm doing this. *Why the hell am I doing this?!*

I hear men talking as I hop down to a crouch. They are speaking Spanish. I dip behind the nearest bush, watching as they go towards an all-black van parked in the driveway. They climb in and pull off immediately.

I see them ride right through the open gates. *The gates are open.* That means freedom, and it also means their guard is down.

When they're gone, that's when I look towards the silver car. It's a Mercedes. I can hear the chiming, as if the keys are still in the ignition, but the car isn't completely started.

I move in closer, looking towards the front of the mansion. The front door is closed and no one is around. Why is the car like this? Someone must be making a quick run in and out.

Well if that's the case, they are most likely here to see Draco. That means he's occupied right now. And that means this car…is *mine.*

My pulse is chaotic, my body vibrating with paranoia and alacrity. I don't know who's watching, and I don't give a fuck if they see me. I am getting the hell out of here. Now, while I have the chance.

Before I can talk myself out of it, my bare feet pound into the gravel, storming for the car.

My breaths are thick and labored as I grip the door handle, yank it open, and clamber inside. The area is vacant as I scan the perimeter. All I can hear is my thundering heartbeat and my heavy breathing.

I glance down and the keys are in the ignition, just as I assumed. I crank the Mercedes up and when the engine effortlessly comes to life, I put it in drive.

Loud Bachata music blares out of the speakers and I gasp, extending my arm and turning it down. My nerves are on end as I turn the wheel while lowering the volume.

"What the fuck?!" A loud voice booms those words from the doorway in Spanish and I whip my head over to the left, peering at the chubby man rushing down the steps.

He has on a brown guayabera shirt with white stitching. The moustache shadowing his upper lip is thick and bushy, just like his eyebrows.

He continues shouting obscenities at me as the tires squeal and I zoom for the gates. But as I get closer, the gates start to close.

"No!" I scream. "No! No! Please!" I'm begging and I don't even know why. Why are they closing? They were just open! I should have just made a run for it. I would have gotten much farther.

I press my foot down on the pedal and the car amps up to thirty miles per hours. I hear the engine grow louder, but the gates are closing in more and more. The black iron is thicker than the gates on the land. This gate is humongous.

But I don't stop.

I won't stop.

I press down on the gas some more, closer and closer, listening to the gates screech as the wheels of the car chase the pavement.

But it's too late.

And I know it.

I slam on the brakes at the last minute, hoping to spare myself, but it's not enough to save me from the collision. Without the seatbelt to save me, my body launches forward and my face smashes into the windshield. I feel my nose crack and my mouth instantly gushes with hot blood.

The horn blares on the car and I hear a man still shouting from a distance.

My body crumples backwards, landing across the seats. My head is woozy; my face hurts. The car's horn is so loud.

I taste so much copper.

I can't move my face.

The passenger door is yanked open and I realize that somehow I'm right beside it. I'm not sure how my body is positioned, but it doesn't matter because in a matter of seconds, I am yanked out and a large hand closes around my throat.

I gasp for air, but the thick hand clamps down tighter. My pulse grows louder as all of the sounds outside of me become inaudible.

The man finally releases my throat and shoves me to the ground. "You stupid fucking bitch! You wrecked my fucking car! Look what the fuck you did!" he barks, "Look at it!" I just lie there, powerless.

I have no fight within me. I hurt myself, but that's nothing compared to what's going to happen to me now.

There is blood everywhere, pooling all around me.

Footsteps stomp on the pavement and before I know it, someone is helping me up. When the person speaks and my hazy state clears up a bit, I realize it's Draco.

I have no idea why hearing his voice gives me so much relief. I tried to run away and he obviously knows it.

I look up, but his eyes aren't on me. They are on the man in front of him.

He asks something in his native tongue and the man answers rapidly, pointing fingers at me. I hear him cursing, shouting.

"Gianna," Draco growls, squeezing my arm tighter. "What the fuck did you do?"

My throat closes in on itself, demanding that I avoid the truth. I look at the chubby man, how he stands there, staring at me with squinty, angry eyes.

He's no good. He's a piece of shit. They are all pieces of shit, but him? He looks like pure garbage.

I want to lie so badly—it's on the tip of my tongue, but I can't. My knees buckle, and I press my fingers to my mouth, hoping it will stop the blood from pouring.

Draco grunts and marches forward with my arm clamped in his large hand.

"You're paying for this fucking damage, Jefe!" the chubby man shouts after him. He follows us into the house and Draco drops me on the sofa when we enter the den.

One of the maids gasps when she sees me, and Draco gives her a direct order.

She complies, dashing away with a quick glance back at me.

"Jefe!" The chubby man rounds the corner, speaking rapidly in their language. "The damage! That's a seventy thousand dollar car, son!"

"I am not your *son*," Draco seethes, stepping forward and getting face to face with him. "I see your fucking car, Morales! I see what the fuck she did!"

"Then you have to pay! She is your *bitch*!"

Draco turns completely and pulls out a gun from the holder on the back of his belt, aiming it at Morales' face. Morales tosses his hands in the air almost immediately, backing away.

He stumbles sideways, hitting the table in the corner and knocking the lamp over.

Draco doesn't give a damn. He still has the gun positioned, ready to take fire. His jaw is tight, his finger wrapped snug around the trigger.

"I was trying to be patient with you, but if you disrespect me under my fucking roof again, I'll show you who my bitch is," he says lowly. Evenly. His accent smooth. "She is my fucking guest so if anyone has the right to call her names, it will be me. Do you fucking understand that?" He says all this in Spanish.

"Yes, Draco. Yes. Just…put the gun down, Jefe. It will not happen again." He drops his hands, motioning for Draco to lower the gun.

Nostrils flared, Draco holds his position—his gun still aimed high, right at the center of Morales's forehead. When the maid walks back in with an icepack and a first aid box, he finally lowers the gun.

I watch all of this from the sofa, sprawled out, motionless. But there's something about this situation that delights me…but I know my delight won't last for long.

"I'll send you money for your car tomorrow. Find Bain and have him drop you back off at your home." Draco places his gun back in the holder and then turns around to look at me.

"Okay, Jefe." Morales walks out, on the hunt for Bain.

I crack a smile—just enough.

Draco notices my amusement and narrows his eyes.

"Is this fucking funny to you?" he snarls, stepping closer and gripping my chin between his fingers. "Look at your fucking face! Your lip is fucking busted! Your nose, broken!" He brings his hand up and clamps his fingers around the bridge of my nose.

"OW! STOP!" I cry out and fling my arms, trying to force him away, but he hardly flinches. He has my nose gripped tight between his fingers, forcing it into place. The cracking and popping sounds much worse than when it went out of place. He squeezes it tight, and I scream even louder until he finally lets up.

He jerks away, and I cup my face, glaring up at him.

He looks down at the maid who is taking out cotton swabs, a needle, and some thread. She rubs my nose with the swabs, ridding it of the blood. Then she picks up a wipe to clean my mouth off. Whatever she uses burns. When I get a whiff of it, I realize it's alcohol.

"You could have fucking died." Draco stands up tall, brows stitched, his gaze heavy on me.

"What is it going to be now?" I croak, peering up at him. "No dinner tonight? No more beach? Or will you make Francesca suck my nipples and play with my hair at the same time?"

Livid, he stomps forward, pushing the maid out of the way and snatching me up. He has my upper arms tight in his hands, that tight jaw even tighter, his eyes blazing with fury.

"You *want* me to fucking kill you, don't you?"

"I don't care what you do to me anymore."

His eyes run all over my face, flashing with what I know is desire. He likes when I talk like this. He hates disobedience, but when I talk back, it triggers something inside him. *Twisted, sick fuck.*

"Well that's just too fucking bad," he grumbles. "I'm not going to kill you. If living here is enough to make you want to die, you're already suffering enough."

He shoves me back down on the sofa and I land with a heavy *oomph*.

The maid picks back up where she started, as if nothing even happened.

"This changes nothing. Be at dinner and in the galería afterwards." He storms away without another word.

I watch him go, and then my gaze travels down to the maid. She merely shakes her head, picking up a cotton swab and swiping my upper lip with it. She's probably thinking I'm the dumbest bitch alive right now, and she's probably right.

But at least I tried to get out of this hellhole.

I could have gotten away with it too if that fat ass slob hadn't shown up. Why the hell was he here anyway?

But furthermore, why hasn't Draco punished me firsthand for this? What the hell is he waiting for? And why do I care?

None of Draco's men show up for dinner. It's only his mother, Francesca, him, and me. Francesca has gotten her spot back beside him, and I couldn't give a shit less. She's way too happy about it.

She eats with her head held high, smiling at Draco whenever he says something in Spanish to his mother.

He hasn't spoken a lick of English since we started eating. He's doing it on purpose. He's trying to make me feel excluded. I honestly don't care. If he's caught on to me by now, he knows I understand everything they're saying. He's just trying to make Francesca feel special tonight—make me look like a discarded toy for now.

His mom has been glancing at me every so often. She's worried. I guess I can understand why. After having to get my upper lip stitched without anything to numb it (and trust me, it hurt like a bitch), I went up to take a shower. Before I got into the shower, I stared at my reflection.

The stitches are right beneath my shattered nose. Draco put it back into place perfectly. I can barely tell there's been damage. It took nearly thirty minutes for it to stop bleeding though.

I don't look completely hideous—I still look like me—minus the stitches and the huge bruise on my forehead. I've covered that bruise with my hair, though.

After dinner is wrapped up, Draco commands me to follow him. Francesca watches us go, sulking in her seat. I don't understand her. Shouldn't she know by now that I'm not enjoying any of this?

"I don't want to go," I call after him, trailing behind.

He glances over his shoulder. When he sees that I've stopped, he comes back with measured steps, walks behind me, and presses his fingertips into my upper back, lightly booting me forward.

"Shut up and keep walking," he demands from behind me.

I scuffle ahead, giving him a sideways glance. It's quiet between us again. Unease sweeps through me when we meet up to the door. I know what this galería means.

This is his inside dungeon.

This is where he destroys his toys.

His pets, rather.

He casually strolls in and steps aside, allowing me to walk ahead of him. When I've stepped in enough, he shuts the door and then walks around me, focused on one of the paintings on the wall.

"I have to say, Gianna," he sighs, unbuttoning his blue shirt. I swallow thickly as he slides out of it. "I'm very disappointed in your behavior today." When the shirt hits the floor, his hard muscles ripple smoothly from the dim lights.

And when he turns around to face me, I finally get the chance to see what's beneath the layers.

His body is toned and cut. His skin looks smooth to the touch, hard in all the right places. It seems he works out to keep in such great shape, but when the hell does he have the time?

He comes to me, his actions fluid beneath the dim lighting. When he's up close, he grips the front of my button-up red blouse and yanks it apart roughly. The buttons fly across the floor, and when my shirt flies open I throw my hands up to cover myself.

He yanks my arms down just as quickly as I brought them up.

"I gave you flowers and a day at the beach. I let you sit alone, hoping I could trust you not to do anything stupid. Because I know you are not a stupid girl, Gianna."

I avoid his eyes as he walks around me, studying my cleavage when he's in front of me again. Reaching around, he unlatches the bra, and I feel his breath run down the bend of my neck.

I can smell his cologne again. It smells expensive…and good. *Ugh.*

When the nude bra falls down, something inside me also collapses. Not this again. *God, what will he do now?*

"You're wondering what's in store…" His lips skim the shell of my ear. "How I will punish you for being so *goddamn* disobedient." His hand wraps around my wrist and he hauls me into him.

"Why don't you just kill me?" I ask. "You said it would be easier to just get rid of me rather than take care of me. I'm a burden to you. Get it over with already. End it," I demand through clenched teeth.

"No. That would be way too easy for me and you know it," he mumbles, and our lips are way too close. He cocks his head to the right. "Don't say anymore. Go upstairs."

I look towards the staircase, blinking slowly, but I don't go. He can't make me. His nostrils flare and he grips my elbow, shoving me towards the stairs. I try and fight him off by squirming but he's too strong for me.

He keeps me wrenched by the elbow until we reach the top of the staircase and then he shoves me away. I stumble forward, but catch myself just in time.

"Skirt and panties off!" he barks with his fists clenched.

I frown up at him. I know the routine already, and even though I'm pissed, my hands are shaky as I pull my skirt down. Even shakier when I manage to get my panties off too.

I'm completely naked in this room again.

In front of this damn bed.

I can feel his eyes running all over me, and when he steps in closer and brings a hand up, I flinch.

He pauses, remaining still for a split second. In no time, he continues with what he was about to do. He tucks a lock of my hair behind my ear. Chills run down my spine from the gesture. It's almost too warm.

"Get on the bed, on your knees, and then face me." I glance up, but his hard brown eyes are already on me.

I climb on top of the bed and then turn around, looking right up at him. With short strides he steps forward. Grabbing my wrist, he pulls my hand up and forces it on his chest. Gradually sliding my palm down his upper body, he lets out a ragged sigh, as if my touch is enough to satisfy him.

I'm confused, but I keep my lips sealed.

When my hands meet the V carved into his waist, he stops me. "Unbuckle my belt."

With unstable hands, I do as told, gaze plummeting. The buckle jingles as I loosen it.

"Unbutton my pants," he demands with a low voice.

I unbutton them, and he slides them down to his ankles. He's wearing a pair of gray briefs, and I see the solid bulge there. He's so hard, and I honestly don't know why.

How can such a "disobedient" girl make a strict man like him so hard? If anything, I should be turning him off for going against his word.

His hand comes down to stroke my cheek. His thumb runs over the area where the stitches are and I wince. When he pulls away, he steps out of his pants and then picks them up.

Yanking out the belt from the loops, he folds it in half in one hand and then tosses the slacks aside.

The thick leather hangs in front of him, and the sight of it causes fear to strike me. I begin to panic, fidgeting on my knees.

He grips my shoulder to keep me still.

"Rest on your stomach, but keep your head up."

He forces me down to my belly. I keep my head up, watching...*waiting*. My heart can't take this. It's pounding so hard. Dangerously hard.

"You're going to suck my cock, Gianna," he murmurs when his lips come closer to me ear. "And as I fuck the shit out of that beautiful mouth of yours, I am going to spank you with this belt. And I will continue to spank you with it until I feel myself coming deep down your fucking throat. After the trouble you've caused—that I had to clean up—you fucking owe me this."

Pressing down on my shoulder, he lowers me until his rock hard bulge is directly in front of my face. When he pulls away, he tugs his briefs down and his cock springs free.

And *oh my fucking goodness.*

He's enormous.

Thick and veiny, with a bulbous tip that would stretch my pussy wider than ever before. He's perfectly hung, and for a second I think about Toni, and how he would envy a man with such a beautiful, massive cock, showing it off to me.

Why couldn't it be small and ugly and pinky-sized?

Why does it have to be so...*big*?

My breathing accelerates when he moves his hips forward and presses the tip on my mouth. My lips are still sealed, but he grips my face, forcing me to spread them apart.

"Resist," he growls, lifting the belt in the air, "and this will end up being worse than it needs to be for you."

I unwillingly open my mouth, and he shoves himself right in. No hesitation whatsoever. I gag from that first thrust, my stomach clenching as I try to claim oxygen.

He puts on a wicked smirk as his smooth, hard flesh draws out and then rams into my mouth again.

Tears form in my eyes as he grips the top of my head with one hand, using the other to lift the belt.

PASSION & VENOM

The leather stings my bare ass, and I yelp around his throbbing cock. But he doesn't stop. He spanks me again.

And again.

And again.

He doesn't let up.

My ass cheeks are scorching, and my throat is getting sore already. My stiches are pulling, almost like they are about to pop, but I can't stop, no matter how much any of this hurts.

He squeezes my hair in his hand, easing up with the belt. He drives harder, quicker, fucking my mouth like the true savage he is.

"Why haven't you learned yet, niñita?" he groans, slamming in. I gag around his length, feeling him deep in my throat. "I am trying to be good to you," he grunts, shuddering, "but you just keep taking what I have to give for granted."

I moan as he grips my hair tighter in his hands. The belt comes up in the air again and he spanks me harder this time. The smack of the leather is so loud that the sound bounces off the walls.

I twitch, gagging and rolling with pain. The belt strikes me all over again, and I beg inside for him to come.

Just come already. Please!

I'll swallow it all if that means the belt will stop.

He whacks me with it again, grinning down at me, still hammering my skull. He then drops the belt and spanks my ass with a heavy hand.

"Look at that sexy ass," he rumbles. His thickness glides deeper. He is balls-deep in my mouth, the tip of his cock lodged in my throat. "Fuck, niñita. That shit feels so fucking good." He spanks my ass again with his large, rough hand, shuddering, and then slamming down as I moan.

His abs are resting on my sore forehead and his cock is much harder now.

He's close.

I can tell.

I ignore all pain and suck like my life depends on it, reaching up to play with his heavy balls. That gets him going. He intensifies his strokes, circling his hips as I mercilessly choke on his dick.

And then it finally happens.

One final plunge and he explodes.

His hot, salty come slithers down and I choke. He pulls out in the nick of time, allowing me to draw in a breath before completely swallowing his thick, hot load.

He steps back sluggishly, glaring down at me. Some of his hair has fallen onto his damp forehead, feathered lightly over his eyes. He watches me swallow it all and then forces me to sit up.

"I should have fucked your pussy instead," he gripes, tugging on my hair. "I should have fucked the shit out of you. Then I'd know you wouldn't try something that stupid again. Because my cock, niñita," he murmurs, bringing me closer by the hair, "is what makes bitches like Francesca so obsessed with me. She hated everything about me…until I fucked some sense into her."

When he pulls away, he puts on a devilish grin. One that makes my skin crawl. He releases my hair and shoves me back, going for his slacks in the corner.

"You will sleep in here tonight. I have something to take care of, but when I get back, you better be here and you better be ready for the rest of your punishment."

The rest of my punishment?! Wasn't this enough? Nearly fucking my throat away? His smirk proves only one thing to me.

He's not fucking around.

He knows I'm not enjoying this, and he also knows I can't protest or resist.

He has me right where he wants me…and I fucking hate him for it.

DAY TWELVE

T*he clock on* the left has just struck midnight.

I haven't slept a wink, though I feel like I should have. I'm exhausted beyond measures, but I'm too afraid to rest. I don't know what he's going to do to me now. After that hateful throat fuck, what else is there to expect?

Maybe it won't be sexual. Maybe it will be something involving guns and knives. I hope so.

Then maybe I can manhandle one and kill him with it.

I rub my raw, bare bottom. It still stings. I pull the blanket over me and curl up.

1:00 A.M. rolls around and that's when I hear distant footsteps.

They are slow, and when the door squeaks on its hinges, my heart sinks. The measured steps continue forward, up the stairs. When I don't hear them anymore, I know he's close.

I can feel his presence.

I nearly stop breathing as I wait for him to say something. Do something.

But he doesn't.

The bed dips, and I hear a long, weary sigh fill the empty space surrounding us. He sounds exhausted.

I remain perfectly still, hoping that if I pretend to be asleep, he'll skip the punishment he owes and spare me all together. I was just in a car wreck, for fuck's sake. Show a little mercy.

When the dip in the bed is gone, I hear him walk around it. He tosses the blanket off of me, and I shut my eyes, but not too tight to make it look forced.

A hand runs over my hips while another forces my shoulder back.

I'm flat on my back, and the hand centers itself between my thighs.

I try not to move, or flinch, or open my eyes.

But it's difficult.

The hand hovers around my pussy, toying with my clit and then dipping a finger into my hole. The finger slides in deep, but still, I hold it in.

I try and adjust myself, acting as if I'm slightly disturbed in my sleep.

I move my leg to the right and turn over, trying to push the hand away with the insides of my thighs, but it doesn't budge.

The hand actually clamps down on my thigh, and I squeeze my eyes tighter as I bury the left half of my face into the cool fabric of the pillow. He forces me onto my back again.

My legs are craned wider apart, the bed dips in the gap between them, and then something hot and wet presses down on my clit.

I gasp, and that gasp alone is what pulls me out of my invented slumber.

I can't hold it in.

Because that something hot is his tongue. It's perfectly wet and as it rubs circles on my clit, my body jolts violently.

When I look down and see his wicked brown eyes locked on me, I feel like I'm in some sort of dream. Maybe a trance, or perhaps even a nightmare.

But nightmares don't feel this good.

Nightmares aren't this damn tempting.

He eats me whole, sucking on my clit as his fingers hatefully fuck me. His tongue applies just enough pressure—not too light or too heavy. My back bows and I moan loudly, clutching the sheets.

"Draco," I breathe out. "Stop. Please."

"Fuck no," he says through full sucks and licks. His tongue slides down and pushes inside me. In and out. Making me wetter than I already am.

When he comes back up, he sticks his fingers inside me again and triggers the sweetest spot of all.

My g-spot.

As he flattens his tongue on my clit and watches me with those fierce brown eyes—I know I won't be able to withhold or outlast him. He grinds his tongue on my clit with gentle force, his fingers running in and out, swirling, and dipping.

I hear my stickiness wrapped around his fingers, and then I hear him groan.

"Oh—fuck." My eyes roll to the base of my skull. My head falls back and a sharp gasp fills the entire galería as it finally happens.

I finally come.

My body is like a fucking bomb.

Every single part of me explodes over and over again, detonating in the best and worst way possible.

The worst because it's him there—doing this to me. I hate him and the tongue that has forced this orgasm right out of me.

The best because…*my fucking word.* I am shattering, writhing, and crumbling and as I push my pussy closer to his face, demanding that he doesn't stop, I feel on top of the fucking world.

Like a queen, really. Having this man eat me.

Knowing what he's done to ruin my life.

In a sense, I feel as if I'm ruling him—forcing him to take what I give, but knowing, for him, that it will never be enough.

In my own fucked-up little head, I own this haunted devil. I am making his tongue, lips, and entire face my bitch, and I don't stop until I see my nectar coating all of him.

When my body finally collapses, I feel absolutely numb.

My lungs work hard, my panting wild.

I can barely move.

I don't remember the last time I came this way.

Wait—have I ever come this way?

So hard? So angrily? So rebelliously?

No, I don't think I have.

Draco pulls up, plants his hands outside my head, and hovers above me.

"That was the rest of your punishment." He watches my eyes, searching for something. I'm not sure what. Bringing his hand up, he sticks his thumb into my mouth and my eyes thin out as we watch each other.

I have the urge to bite it, but I'm stuck.

On his eyes.

On him.

When he presses his thumb into the print of my bottom teeth to wrench my lips apart, he lowers his face, and consumes me whole.

His lips are soft and greedy, the kiss heightening sensual parts of me that it shouldn't.

His hard cock rubs across my thigh, and he lets out a throaty groan. My core clenches as he grabs my wrists with his hands, pinning me to the bed.

"Look at you," he rasps when he breaks the kiss. "So fucking ready for me. I should fuck your pussy while it's so soft and wet, but I won't. Because that's exactly what you want from me. Your pussy is hungry for my cock, but like I said before, only *obedient* little girls can have it."

I writhe beneath him. "Just get it over with," I mutter.

He vibrates with deep laughter, pulling away and sitting up straight. He climbs off the bed with a massive hard on, adjusting himself as much as possible.

"Juanita told me you don't have a concussion from the crash. You're tired. Go to sleep, Gianna."

He walks around the bed and takes the stairs slowly. I watch him go without looking back, and I don't bother moving a bit.

I don't hear a door open or close.

He's still around. I hear him moving things down there. I hear water run and then stop.

He's about to paint. He's not leaving this room, probably for the rest of the night.

I sigh and stare up at the vaulted ceiling.

My body is in dire need of rest. My womanhood is glowing and I'm way too relaxed right now. I am ashamed of myself…again.

What the hell is happening?

I hate this man. *I hate this man!*

I do.

I hate the way he makes me feel.

He's confusing my body, but he won't get to my mind.

My heart still hates him. My brain as well.

As long as I have them on the same side, my satisfied pussy is just a confused organ that doesn't know any better.

He will not win me over like he did Francesca.

I will use my body as much as I can, but my heart and mind will keep their distance from that vicious man.

I don't get the welcoming warmth of the sun this morning.

This room doesn't have any windows.

My eyelids pull apart and all I see is the vaulted white ceiling.

It's quiet in here. I don't hear any movement. I sit up and push out of bed, tiptoeing towards the railing. I look down, but don't see anything.

I go back to pick up my panties and make my way down half the stairs. I bend over to look where his canvas is.

He's not here.

Does that mean I'm free to go?

I rush back up the stairs and sit on the edge of the bed for a moment to think. I check the alarm clock and it's 7:15 a.m. I should probably go and get changed for breakfast. I bet that's where he'll be, and he's probably waiting for me to arrive.

I gather my skirt and shoes and then jog down the stairs.

My torn shirt is on the table in the center of the room. I pick it up and slide my arms into it. Wrapping the ends of it around, I make sure to conceal the private parts of me before walking out. I don't know who's lurking about.

If Bain is around, I damn sure don't need him to see me like this.

I walk to the door and pull it open. It screeches a bit, but I keep moving. The hallway is clear when I make it up the first set of stairs. I rush down and when I pass the dining room, I'm relieved to know it's empty.

I hear the chefs and butlers in the kitchen. I can smell something sweet and something salty. It all smells really good.

As I make my way down the corridor, that's when I spot someone standing a short distance away.

And it's just my fucking luck that it's Bain.

He's standing in the other kitchen with an apple in his hand. When he spots me through the corner of his eye, he turns fully, narrowing his cold gaze.

I walk faster to get to the staircase.

He stares even harder. He even takes a step forward.

I fucking hate that man.

I hate how he stares at me like I'm a piece of meat. If he doesn't stop this soon, I may just end up ratting him out. I'll say he touched me. Maybe Draco will get so pissed that he'll fire him.

Shit. Who am I kidding? Bain is clearly his right hand man. He handles everything from what I've observed. Whenever Draco needs something done, he sends Bain first. He trusts Bain too much to let a girl like me interfere.

Patanza steps up to his side and they both watch me ascend the steps. When I can no longer see them, I release a ragged breath. I know they're talking about me, and probably Draco too.

I'm practically undone. A torn shirt and no shoes on my feet. I'm sure my hair is a disheveled mess and my face is fucked up from that damn crash. I'm too afraid to even check the mirror.

By the soreness alone, I know I'm not very appealing to the eye right now.

I enter my bedroom quietly, shutting the door behind me and tossing all of my things in the recliner. When I look towards the vanity, I notice the chocolate cosmos are still there.

I don't know why I thought they'd be gone. I don't deserve them.

They still have life, and their fragrance has permeated this bedroom.

My mouth twitches as I stare at them. I walk closer to them, running my finger across one of the petals. I then pull one out and sniff it. It smells good. So good that it relaxes me.

Tucking the flower away, I walk to the closet and pull down an outfit. For a split second I realize I'm wondering where Draco is. When did he leave last night? Why didn't he actually *punish* me?

I have to admit that even though he was there, I slept like a baby. He didn't bother me again after forcing that orgasm out of me. I would remember.

He painted for some time. I dozed off after about an hour, when I realized he was actually leaving me alone.

I have to say…it was the best sleep I've had since being here.

In this bedroom, I sleep with one eye open. I make sure that when those footsteps go past my door, my guard is up and I am ready to pounce.

But last night, the man that lurks this very door was only a few feet away from me. He had no reason to sneak by. And I had nothing to fear other than another form of punishment.

No one else was going to intrude. He would have put a stop to it before it even happened…and something about that made me feel safe.

Fuck me. Safe while being held captive?

What kind of shit is that?

I think I'm becoming just as twisted as they are.

After my shower, I brush my hair and it collects around my heart-shaped face. The bruise on my forehead is darker, and the stitches above my lip are red around the edges.

I look battered.

There are still dark circles beneath my eyes and I can tell I've lost some weight but I feel…better. Hell, why couldn't I lose these pounds before my wedding?

After last night, something has shifted, and I hate that I don't feel as much weight as I once did.

I hate that I am starting to feel sheltered.

It shouldn't be this way.

But he makes it so hard to see it otherwise.

Wicked bastard.

This is probably part of his plan. This is exactly what he wants.

For me to feel protected by him. For me to call on him when I feel threatened. For me to reach out to him when I need something, like a day at the beach or a fucking alarm clock just so I can make it to breakfast on time.

He wants me to need him.

He wants me to *crave* him.

He wants me to rest on my knees and give myself to him.

He wants me…all of me, or nothing at all.

This twisted game he's playing confuses me. What in the hell does he see in me anyway? I am not the woman he should want.

I am the woman with a wrath he should be afraid of.

I waltz out of the bathroom with a towel wrapped around me, running a finger over my sore stitches. As I pick up my head, I spot a figure by the chocolate cosmos and I freeze.

The sunlight from the window across the room reveals her, and when she turns halfway, she grimaces. Francesca.

"Why the hell are you in my room?" I demand, scowling.

"You still call this *your* room," she scoffs, turning in my direction and folding her arms. "This room you're in is only temporary. You'll be gone soon."

My eyelids grow thin. "Get the fuck out of my room," I growl.

She smirks. "You think you're winning him over, don't you?" I don't speak. I don't have to answer to her. When she takes a step closer, I take one back, squaring my shoulders. When she takes note of my hostile stance, she freezes, and then she laughs. "I can't figure out why he let you sleep in there," she mutters. "You're no better looking than I am and I can give him so much more."

"You're afraid of him," I bite out. "I'm not. That's the difference."

She looks me over. "You should be."

"Well, I'm not. Now get the hell out of my room."

Her irritating laughter fills the room and then she turns with her hands in the air. "I can't wait to see how *he* breaks you too. You're not afraid now, but trust me…that will change. You think you're safe…but you have no fucking idea. Watch your back, bitch."

She's out of the bedroom before I know it, the door slamming behind her. I swallow thickly, focusing on the flowers. There is one that has been pulled out. It's resting on top of the vanity and it's petals have been plucked.

My eyebrows narrow as I rush forward and pick up the petals and then the stem, tossing it in the trash. But it's when I return to the room that I see something.

A carved image of a skull. It's small, but the dust surrounding it is fresh. She did this while I was showering. It has been imprinted in the wood vanity, and it looks just like the skull on Draco's ring.

I look towards the door, and then back at the window.

Gooseflesh rises on my skin. My heart pounds much harder.

I rush to the closet for something to wear and get dressed quickly. I toss my hair up into a bun while pulling the door open and pacing my way out.

Draco is standing in the dining room when I make it there. His hands are in the front pockets of his brown slacks as a younger man in a white button-down shirt speaks to him.

When I meet the unknown man's eyes, a sharp gasp escapes me and both of them look my way when they hear it.

Kevin. Toni's driver.

I freeze solid in my tracks and Draco turns fully to look me, pulling his hands out of the pockets. Kevin is sporting a casual smirk, his eyes mellow as if he's never done any wrong.

"Gianna," Draco calls, cocking a brow. "Have a seat. Breakfast will be served in a minute."

I barely nod my head, walking around the opposite side of the table to reach my chair. I feel Kevin watching me.

Draco continues talking to him in Spanish, and I'm surprised to hear Kevin exchanging responses in Spanish as well.

He's an all-American man. Blonde hair and a clean face. I asked him once if he could speak Spanish when we were in a fender bender with a Hispanic woman and he flat out told me no. He lied. I guess I shouldn't be surprised to know that.

He's a liar. And a conspirator.

Sweat beads up on the back of my neck and my forehead as I look towards Mrs. Molina. She's knitting away as she waits, but she glances up once before looking away. She doesn't want to be involved today. Maybe she knows I slept in the galería.

Is she against it now?

The idea of Draco and me…?

"Don't worry about it right now. Come join us for breakfast." Draco's voice fills the dining room as he caps Kevin's shoulder.

"I am pretty damn hungry." Kevin's lips stretch to smile.

When Draco turns and walks towards his chair, Kevin comes in my direction and takes the seat right beside me.

Francesca plops down in the chair beside Mrs. Molina moments later and when we are all gathered at the table, the butlers come out with hot food.

I remain quiet as Draco and Kevin continue talking amongst themselves, realizing that Francesca is now the least of my worries.

With my fork clutched in hand, I breathe as evenly as possible, staring down at my omelet and the coffee on the side.

As they speak cordially, I focus on the knife inside my cloth. It's nestled there, and I'm sure Draco hasn't even given it a second thought that I have a knife in reach.

My heart is drumming. My eyes feel tight. My palms are clammy around the silver fork, but I use it to cut into the omelet and then chew slowly, pretending I'm okay.

Something starts to ring and Draco pauses on his meal, looking down.

"You all keep eating. I have to take this," Draco murmurs as his phone continues to vibrate. He fishes it out, pushes out of his chair, and then leaves the dining room to go down a hallway.

We hear him answer it, but everyone continues eating. Everyone but me.

"So, Gia, it's been a while. How are you liking it here?" Kevin's voice booms and the sound of it makes my entire body tense up.

I ignore him, picking at my breakfast.

"Look, I know you're surprised to see me, and I know you want to hate me," he chuckles, "but what Toni failed to realize when he hired me is that I'm a floater.

I work for whoever pays me the most. No hard feelings or anything. It was just business." He holds his hands out in a nonchalant gesture. "My orders were to cause a distraction and let his men take care of the rest." He holds his hands up in the air, carelessly shrugging. "You can't really be upset about something you couldn't control." He chews some more and then picks up his coffee. "The way I see it, you got lucky. You didn't need to be married to that jackass anyway."

Before he takes a sip, he says, "Toni was a fucking asshole. Fucking stupid, too. I wasn't going to last long with him anyway. You should be glad you're here. Better off with Jefe than that dipshit. I can't imagine how you feel though. I mean, you hate me and I know it, but you have to hate *him* more. He's the one who called the hit." His lips purse to fight a smile as he side eyes me.

He takes a sip of his coffee.

I watch him swallow it with a smirk, my knee bouncing.

His hand is on the table.

I don't hesitate on the urge that sweeps through me.

I pick up the knife in front of me and I don't waver. I stab the sharp end of the blade through the hand he has resting on the table.

Francesca and Mrs. Molina gasp sharply.

Kevin roars with agony and I shoot out of my chair, but I don't run. I refuse to run this time. I want him to look me in the eye and know why this was done. It should be much worse than this for him. After what he did to Toni, setting all that shit up, and then pistol-whipping me.

He should suffer.

"I fucking hate you! Toni trusted you! I trusted you!" I scream.

I take his cup of hot coffee and toss it at his face. He wails even more from the burn, but during all of this, I have forgotten that Mrs. Molina and Francesca are still sitting across from me.

They stare at me with wide, bewildered eyes. Ignoring them, I reach over for Kevin's knife and aim right for Kevin's throat as he tries yanking the other knife out.

But I don't make it in time.

A hand clamps down on my wrist and then I'm yanked away and forced down in my chair.

I look up, meeting heavy, hard brown eyes.

Draco's nostrils are flared, his fists clenched as he grips the handle of the knife.

"What the fuck is your problem?!" Kevin shouts, still struggling to pull the knife out. "Stupid, miserable fucking *bitch*!"

Draco turns and snatches the knife out of his hand, and Kevin howls, clutching his bloody hand to his chest.

"Mama, take Kevin to Juanita to see what she can do for him." Juanita is the maid that stitched me up. "Francesca, get the fuck out." Draco's tone is way to calm. Eerily calm.

Both Francesca and Mrs. Molina hop up out of their chairs. They look at me once more, stunned.

Mrs. Molina demands Kevin to get up and follow her and when they are all out of the dining room and the door is closed, Draco focuses on me. His face is as hard as stone. His eyebrows are stitched together, his lips pressed tight, jaw ticking.

He seizes my body and tosses me over his shoulder.

"Put me down!" I shout.

He storms towards the french doors, stalking out of the dining room and hurrying down the corridor.

I expect him to go towards the galería but he doesn't. He takes a sharp right turn and opens a wide black door.

He walks in, slams it behind him, and then spins around.

He slams my back down on an unknown bed. I don't know where we are, but it's a large room with navy blue walls and a massive California king bed. The bed is covered in white sheets, and I notice a portrait on the wall behind him.

There's a man. He looks just like Draco.

My jeans are unbuttoned and yanked down, and then my panties.

"Get off of me!" I grimace, shoving a hand on his face.

He ignores me, tossing my hand away and shoving my shirt and bra up to reveal my breasts. He clutches my breasts in hand and then his mouth wraps around my nipple, sucking fiercely.

I gasp and my pussy clenches tight. I yank on his hair by the roots to wrench him away. He releases my nipple, but that was stupid of me to do.

He unbuckles his belt, undoes his button, and then his massive cock springs free.

"Why'd you try to kill him?" he demands, pressing his cock on my entrance. My wrists are now clasped in his large hands and glued to the bed.

"Because he's a backstabber. He was a part of your fucked-up plan to kill Toni!" I spit, scowling up at him.

"And that means stab him in my house and leave his blood all over my fucking table?" He grabs my chin. "I brought him here for a reason."

"Why would you invite him to breakfast after what he did?"

"Because you're right. He's a backstabber and I don't like backstabbers. Or liars."

I'm confused now. I narrow my eyes. "What are you talking about?"

"I brought him here so I can *kill* him."

"Over a lie?!"

"No. For my safety and yours. He's looking for more money. He's here to kill me." He pauses very briefly. "You don't know this, but there is a warrant out for my arrest. No one knows where the fuck I am unless I let him or her know. And I let him know because I know what he wants. He wants the reward for my capture. Dead or alive, they want me."

"You're wanted?" I pant, easing up on my resistance.

"The reward is for three million dollars." He shrugs one shoulder. "What man can resist?"

My eyes stretch wide and the back of my head lands on the bed again. I ease up, only slightly.

"You injured him for me—put his guard down for now. You'll make killing him a lot easier. Not that I needed help in the first place. He's a fucking idiot for coming into my home with no back up." The tip of his cock presses in and a harsh breath shoots past my lips. "And seeing you so angry—so eager to get rid of a man that betrayed you— has made me too fucking hard to not fuck you right now. It makes me wonder how far you'd go to try and get rid of me." His smirk makes my throat feel thick. "I've been patient with you, but I won't pass up this opportunity. I'm done fucking around, Gianna. I want you *now*."

His hot mouth presses on the crook of my neck, and with no hesitation at all, he slides his cock into me.

My breath is bated as he clutches my wrists in hand and focuses on my face. He watches me—holds me—and then he slams inside me. I feel myself stretching wider for him, my walls holding him snug.

He moves rapidly, my ass at the edge of the bed, thrusting quickly between my thighs. His grunts are heavy, and as his lips press on the bend of my neck, I sigh.

The sound of slapping skin ricochets off the blue walls, and my back bows even more.

I hear Kevin shouting out in pain from a faraway distance, and something about hearing that and having Draco inside me tips me right over the edge.

It gives me a sense of power.

Control.

"I have wanted to make you mine for a long time, *niñita*," he rasps in my ear. He lowers his head and his mouth closes around one of my nipples again.

"Oh, God," I whimper, pulsing around him. It's been so long since I've had this. So long. And it feels way too good.

A mixture of guilt and pleasure swims through my bloodstream. I hate myself for this—indulging in such a sinful act. I hate myself for not resisting.

Draco shouldn't have me like this, right in the palm of his hand. He shouldn't have gotten in this easily, but I find myself digging my nails into his hips and welcoming him in. Forcing him deeper.

My fingernails glide up, and then scatter down his back, leaving marks that I know won't fade for days.

"Fuck, Gianna," he groans with a dip of his hips. His mouth is less than an inch away from mine. "He never deserved you," he murmurs. "No one on this earth deserves you but *me*."

I start to protest against his words, my hands dropping to shove against his chest, but he grips my forearms, slams them to the bed again, and then places his mouth on mine.

His tongue thrashes through my lips, while his cock drives harder and deeper, bringing me higher—filling me up with forbidden ecstasy.

He pulls both hands away, cupping the back of my neck with one while using the other to press his thumb down on my clit. He applies just the right amount of

PASSION & VENOM

pressure as he drives his cock slower.

The feeling is too much.

My body is overheated with lust, desire, and shame.

My heart doesn't know what to do.

And my mind... *fuck*. My mind is so lost. So confused.

I swore he wouldn't get to my heart or my mind...but I was *so fucking wrong*. He's forced his way in and I don't know how to come back from this.

I can't stop it—he feels so amazing.

"Your pussy feels so good wrapped around me," he grumbles against my lips. "I can tell you've wanted to feel my cock. I know this is exactly what you needed in order to finally fucking behave." His hand slides up and locks around my throat. His grip isn't tight at all, but the gesture alone is enough to make me explode.

He's still stroking with his hot brown eyes on mine.

His brows are dipped and his lips are close to mine. He's drawing me in, soaking up all that I can give. I am in my most vulnerable state.

Pussy aching.

Body jolting.

My moans echoing across the room.

I need to release. I need to let go. I'm aching so much.

I want him to make me cum so bad it hurts.

And as he slams inside me, squeezes my face in his hand, and crushes my lips with his, it finally happens. He gives me what I want and I don't hold back.

My legs quake harder than they ever have before. I cry out, gripping him tighter, squeezing as if my life depends on it.

He's groaning, watching me unravel, and before I know it, he stills, and his face falls into the crook of my neck.

"Fuucckkk," he growls, holding on tight to my wrists. "Tight, wet fucking pussy." He says this with his lips to my collarbone. All in Spanish.

I pant raggedly as he rests on top of me. We stay this way for longer than a minute, catching our breath.

The door creaks and both of us look towards it at the same time. We see long, curly dark hair with bright honey streaks and I know it's Francesca. The door shuts so fast that we don't even get the chance to see her face. All we see is her leaving.

Wait…was she watching? Did she walk in on us?

"Francesca!" Draco barks. "Nosy fucking bitch," he mutters.

Rage ignites my spirit knowing he's probably done this to her before too.

Tears swarm my eyes as I stare up at the ceiling, but I don't let them fall.

I shove him off of me and then scramble for my panties and jeans. I put them on rapidly, avoiding his eyes. My insides are all fucked up. I feel like I need to vomit.

"What the hell are you doing, Gianna?"

"Leaving." My voice is hurried as I pull my shirt down and adjust my bra.

I rush for the door, but Draco chases after me, catching my elbow and slinging me around before I can escape.

"You're not leaving yet." His voice is grave. "We have something to take care of. Kevin, remember?"

"I don't want to see you kill him."

He smirks, raking his fingers through his hair. "Yes, you do. Don't lie to yourself."

"I'm tired of seeing blood," I whisper, staring up at him.

His face remains even. "While you're under my roof, seeing blood will become a normal thing."

"What are you going to do to him?"

Draco releases me and then walks away to pick up his pants. He adjusts his red tie and then tucks his black shirt in. When he comes towards me again, he grips my hand in his and then pulls the door open.

"Whose room is that?" I ask when we're in the hall and he strings me along.

He side eyes me before responding. "It's the room I stayed in as a teenager…before my father died." He pauses. "He let me stay in it because it's close to the galería. It's sacred now. Private. I have a bedroom upstairs that I use more."

Oh.

"What are you going to do to him?" I ask again as he drags me along.

"You'll see," is all he says.

I clamp my mouth shut because the truth is I want to see this happen. I want Kevin to die. That traitorous bastard will keep on lying and betraying for the next big buck. All he sees is dollar signs. He's a greedy fucker.

He needs to go out much harder than Toni did.

And when he does, I want to be a witness. I want to see blood spill from his head and through his lips just like it did from Toni's. I want to see the regret on his face, just like Toni before he was taken away from me.

If that makes me just as heartless as Draco, then so be it.

I no longer care about helping the people who have only put me in harm's way.

DAY TWELVE
CONTINUED

We walk past the pool and he takes a left. My hand is still in his. My heart is racing. I'm somewhat terrified, thinking about what he could do to kill Kevin.

We walk for about two minutes before reaching our destination. There are two wooden doors that most likely lead down to the basement.

They are close to the ground—doors that must be pulled open. Draco releases my hand and bends down to yank the doors open. They hit the sides with a loud *thump*.

He dusts off his hands and then glances over his shoulder at me. "Let's go."

He starts down the steps. I watch him disappear and then inch forward. It's so dark down there. How can he even see?

I follow suit, though. I know I can't back out. He wants me to see this—and frankly, deep down, I need to know what he does to him. I walk down the steps quickly and when I round the corner, that's when I see the single light hanging from the ceiling. It has a blue tint to it, making Draco appear even deadlier as he stands across the room.

My eyes dip over to Bain, who is standing with his arms crossed in front of him and a gun in his hand. He watches me very carefully, one brow cocked, those beady, ugly eyes of his repulsing me.

In front of him is Kevin. He's on his knees, his head hung low. There's blood dripping from his left hand—the one I stabbed. I'm guessing Juanita didn't mend him.

I hold my breath, looking up at Draco. His steps are slow and residual as he walks my way. When he's close, he threads his fingers through my hair and then leans in to put his lips close to the shell of my ear.

His arm lifts, and he points towards a few barrels that are close to the light. "You see those barrels?"

"Yes." I finally breathe.

"Can you guess what's inside of them?"

"I don't know…what?"

"*Acid.*"

"Acid?" I gasp.

"Yes. Hydrofluoric acid. And that's where little old Kev will be sleeping tonight. In a barrel full of acid, never to be found again."

My blood runs cold. I stare at the solid black barrel, my heart sinking down. Bain grips Kevin's arm and drags him towards the middle of the room, and then he forces him down on his knees again.

I watch, horrified, as Draco walks away from me, grabs a pair of chemical resistant gloves hanging on the wall, and then slides them over his fingers.

"Stay back, niñita," he murmurs.

I take a leap back, but he walks closer to a begging Kevin. There is gray tape covering his mouth, but those eyes are frantic.

Draco shifts to the right and takes the lid off of one of the barrels.

There is a cool smile on his lips, one that sends repeated shivers up and down my spine. I take a look around the basement again.

It's full of junk that's placed against the walls behind me, but this one space where we stand is clear. Probably for shit like this to happen. For him to destroy, kill, and make people disappear.

Kevin looks at me and muffles something behind the gray tape.

I narrow my eyebrows. "You should take the tape off. Let him get his last words out before he's gone," I suggest, peering up at Draco.

I notice Bain's shoulders hike up as if I'm wrong for making suggestions. He looks at Draco, waiting for him to send me backlash, but that's not what happens.

"You're right," Draco says, and then he puts his gaze on Bain. "Take the tape off."

Bain clomps forward, glaring at me once before ripping the tape off of Kevin's mouth. Kevin's lips are red around the edges, and he clenches his jaw, giving a small glare at Bain.

"Stand him up," Draco demands.

Bain yanks Kevin up, but Kevin has his eyes on me right now.

"You're trusting him now?" he interrogates, grimacing. "Toni is probably flipping in his fucking grave."

My mouth twitches. "Toni isn't in a grave. It's because of you that his body is dumped somewhere that I'll never be able find."

"Yeah, but why do you think that is? It's not my fault he's dead. If you're going to point fucking fingers, point them at the fucker that kidnapped you in the first fucking place!"

My eyes shift over to Draco. His demeanor hasn't changed one bit, but he is pacing slowly now, absorbing every word.

He says nothing at all, which gives Kevin the ammunition to keep going.

"He had someone come to me and hand me $80,000 in cash. I wasn't going to pass that shit up. Toni was only paying me $19,000 every two months. That shit wasn't cutting it for me. Why wouldn't I go for the eighty grand and then get more for killing *this* bastard? I know that's why I'm down here."

I shrug. "Your lust for money is why you're in the position you're in now."

"And your greedy little pussy hungering for motherfuckers like Trigger Toni and Draco Molina is the reason your life is fucking ruined and will never be the same again! You get off on shit like this. You want a man with power, but what you fail to realize is that all great things collapse. If it seems too good to be true, chances are it probably is. And you stand there, looking at me as if I'm the bad guy?" He scoffs, and a smile weaves its way across his lips. "No, if anyone is to blame, it's *you*, Gia. *You* put yourself in this position the day you decided to fuck motherfuckers like your dead husband and then *him*."

Kevin spits in Draco's direction. Draco glares down at the spit, and then he flicks his fingers, gesturing for Bain to bring him forward.

His patience has dwindled. He's done listening.

Kevin jerks and twists, resisting, but Draco grabs hold of him by the back of the neck.

"Fucking bitches! All of you!" Kevin shouts.

Draco's hand moves up to grip the base of Kevin's head, those blonde strands clasped between his fingers, and then he shoves his face down, straight into the barrel.

Kevin's entire head has been dunked in acid, and I hear the sizzle as it happens. His garbled screams are terrifying. And as Draco pulls up, revealing his face, I cover my mouth and back away, bumping into the banister.

His skin has melted off his face. His eyes…they're gone. There is only blood and bone, and the sight of it sends me spinning around to face the wall.

Kevin's screeches have been silenced.

All I hear is his head being dunked back into the acid, and then Bain chuckling as Draco grunts with annoyance, shoving the rest of his body into the barrel.

The sizzling noise is louder now.

I even smell the melting flesh.

I dry heave, clutching the banister. My throat is thick with disgust, my heart heavy in my chest. I grip the banister tighter, and then, moments later, a hand touches my shoulder.

I look up at Draco.

He runs his eyes up and down.

I start to step away from him, but he catches me, draping an arm around my shoulders.

"It's done. Let's go."

He spins me around and we walk back up the stairs. I hear a loud grunt and a heavy thunk and I get the urge to look back to see what Bain is doing, but I don't. I keep my eyes forward and my words to myself.

I have never seen anything like that before. I thought he would use a knife or a gun. But no. He didn't waste a bullet on his traitorous ass. He used his own two hands and in less than a minute, Kevin was gone.

I want to be pleased by this—knowing Kevin is gone—but his words ring in my head. They repeat over and over again, and I can't believe I'm acting like it never even occurred.

Toni is gone because Draco wanted him dead.

How can I be with Draco, knowing that he is still the man that slaughtered my husband?

In a sense, I should still want him dead.

But if Draco dies, there will be no one to protect me at all.

I would die here…and I refuse to die. If that means making the enemy my ally, then so be it.

We make it upstairs and as soon as we meet at the top, I suck in all the fresh air that I can, cleansing my mind and body.

Draco finally pulls away from me and turns to his left.

"This way." He cocks his head.

I watch him for several seconds before following suit. He walks across a brick pathway, and then leads the way to a gated area.

The fence is painted a glossy white, and inside it are the chocolate cosmos he sent up to my room.

There's at least half an acre of them. I can smell them when the wind blows, and they smell warm and welcoming.

For a split second I forget all about the ugly that just happened and absorb the exquisiteness before me. Draco pushes the gate of the fence open and strides in. He makes his way across the thin path that's around the bloomed flowers and then bends down.

Pulling out a pocketknife, he slices the stem of one of the flowers and then stands up, inhaling it. A sigh falls through his full lips as he lowers the flower and then points his gaze up at me.

"Come here, Gianna."

I walk slowly. When I'm near, he turns and straightens his back. His hand reaches up, and he tucks my hair behind my ear. I flinch, but ease up almost instantly when I realize he isn't trying to hurt me.

"Are you glad he's gone?"

I remain silent for a moment. "I thought I would be...but I...I don't know. I didn't think you'd *torture* him that way."

"Wasn't torture," he replies, looking down at the large bed of flowers. "He died quickly, in my opinion. It's life, niñita. Eat or be eaten. Kill or be killed."

"Is that something your father taught you?"

"No," he says, and then he smirks. "It's actually something *your* father taught *me*."

I gape at him, not daring to pull my line of vision away. "If you were so close to Daddy, why didn't I ever see you? Why can't I remember you?"

"Because he didn't bring me around you. I came and left with my father. The only time I could come was during the summer because of school. During summer, you were hardly there. He used to send you to camps to keep you away from the business and violence. Your father and mine worked together often...until mine passed away and I had to take over."

I lower my gaze to the day-old scruff on his jaw.

"Like I said before...he is the only reason you are still alive."

"How can you remember me if you hardly saw me?"

"Oh, I saw you more times than I could count when I used to visit. Portraits, mainly. When I first saw you, it was in person though." He laughs silently. "You wouldn't remember. You were clueless—too focused on school and being a good girl like Daddy said."

I roll my eyes, looking down.

"He never wanted anything to happen to you."

"But you decide to have my husband murdered and then kidnap me," I snap.

"I didn't fucking know who Toni was marrying. I heard the news, heard it was happening in Mexico, set the shit up, and there was no turning back after that. I refuse to look weak or to lose authority in front of my men, no matter who I'm dealing with. Toni came into my territory thinking he was safe. I had to be quick— quicker than that motherfucker." He grips the stem of the flower in hand, his eyebrows bunching together as he breathes through flared nostrils. "The men that work for me can be very fucking stupid. No one knew how close your father and me were. None of them, but they did know I did exclusive business with Nicotera before he died. That's why they didn't report a name to me. They didn't know who he was, or that he even had a daughter, and Lion wanted it that way. In all honesty, I didn't give a fuck who Trigger Toni was marrying. I assumed his wife was just some bitch that was like him. Greedy and fucking full of herself. I needed to see you for myself—see what all you knew—and then figure out what to do with you."

"But then you realized I am Gianna Nicotera."

"A fucking Nicotera," he scoffs, shaking his head. "What were the fucking odds?"

"You weren't expecting him to marry someone like me?"

"I wasn't expecting anyone that worked with Lion to get anywhere near his damn daughter. He was strict about that, but Toni clearly broke that commandment. Fucking pig. That was his problem. He didn't know how to fucking listen."

My eyebrows dip as I look up at him. "He was still my husband."

"For less than a fucking hour. And does it look like I give a shit?"

"You should," I retort. "I loved him."

"What did I tell you about love?" He clasps my chin in his hand. "Love is fucking useless, Gianna. Get rid of the fucking idea. It won't get you anywhere while you're around here."

I narrow my gaze. "Why do you hate him so much?"

My question obviously triggers something within him. He rapidly pulls away from me, looking me over. He then extends his arm to hand me the flower.

I frown down at it, but I take it, hoping it will get an answer out of him.

It doesn't. And his silence really ticks me off.

His cellphone rings and he finally pulls his eyes away from me, fishing it out of his pocket. He answers right away, lifting a finger in the air at me before walking off and speaking in his native language.

I sigh and lower myself to my knees. I twirl the flower by the stem, getting a whiff of it. They all smell so lovely.

Such beautiful flowers. I don't get how all this beauty can survive around people so rotten.

I lay the loose flower down and then bend down to pluck another one out.

PASSION & VENOM

I pluck out three more, laying them on top of each other, but when I come across the fourth one, my finger hits something hard.

I jerk away rapidly, waiting to see some kind of creature or animal pop out.

But nothing happens. No movement. Nothing.

I glance at Draco. His back is facing me. His tone is calm.

I lean forward again and dip my fingers beneath the petals of the flowers. When I feel the hard surface again, I run my fingers over it. Maybe it's a weapon... a gun, hopefully?

Nope.

As my fingers continue to glide, I realize it's roundish and smooth. My hand clasps around the object and I yank it up.

When I see what it is, something between a gasp and a screech shoots in the air. Shocked, I jump up to my feet, releasing the object and backing away. It lands on the ground with a thunk, but my feet don't stop moving backwards.

I stumble into the fence and Draco hears the commotion, turning his head to peer over his shoulder. His eyes are hard.

Mine shift back over to the skull that's lying on the ground. Its eye sockets are dark and hollow, the teeth formed in an eerie sneer that I will never be able to get out of my head.

My heart thuds against my rib cage and I step to the left.

The skull is sideways, facing me, but I notice an imprint on the back.

Letters.

I drop to my knees with shaky hands and roll the skull onto its face.

The letters are *TTR*.

A shadow hovers above me and then the skull is snatched up. Draco holds it by the empty sockets, studying every aspect of it.

"I see you found one of my most prized possessions."

I swallow the bile in my throat. "Prize," I whisper. I wobble to my feet. "Whose skull is that?"

A smirk sweeps across his lips. "Did you read the initials?"

"Initials?"

TTR.

"Who is TTR?"

He holds the skull by the back of the head and puts it right in my face. "Take a wild guess. It may be familiar to you if you actually look at it."

TTR…TTR…TTR…

"It's someone you knew…but not as well as you'd like to think."

I pick my head up rapidly and glare at him.

"Toni?" I whisper. "Toni!"

"Trigger Toni Ricci." He releases a throaty chuckle. "I scalped his head myself. Scooped the eyeballs out with a spoon. Cut off the skin with some of my best knives. Had some of my men clean it down to the bone and then bring it back here."

"You are a sick fucking bastard!" I shove him against the chest and then smack a hand across his cheek. The action is so swift that I don't have much time to process what I've just done.

Draco doesn't react much, but his nostrils do flare at the edges and his head dips. A shadow is casted over the top half of his face. His lips are thin and pressed flat.

"Why would you bring that here? Why would you bring *me* here? Why would you mutilate him like that and then shove it in my face!"

"He should be glad I didn't do worse!"

"Are you so fucking crazy and evil that you have to keep a man's skull over a little bit of fucking territory?! Is that what this is about?!"

He takes a step closer, looking me right in the eyes. "You have no fucking idea what this is about," he grumbles through clenched teeth. "You are too fucking blind, thinking he was perfect. Thinking he actually fucking *loved* you," he spits out.

"He did love me," I fume, rage filling my voice.

"That's what he wanted you to believe." Draco's head barely shakes. "This skull? It's a reward for myself for finally getting rid of that piece of shit. He was a fucking disgrace."

"Just tell me what he did!"

He steps back, bends down, and places the skull beneath the flowers again. When he's upright, he mutters, "I don't have to tell you shit, Gianna."

"You're a fucking monster. *You* are the disgrace. I can't believe I let you fuck me," I spit at him.

"You know why you let me fuck you. You can't resist me. You can't deny me, even if you try to. You know that I fucking *own* you and that you aren't going anywhere anytime soon. I don't answer to you, Gianna. You answer to me." He takes a sly step forward. "And the next time you talk that way to me, I will be sure to keep your skull as my keepsake too. Now get your ass back to your room and shut the fuck up before you piss me off."

He has a stern finger pointed at me. Those dark brown eyes seem to have grown multiple shades darker, even with the sun directly on us. He doesn't let up, and I don't want to run away, but I refuse to stay here.

Next to Toni's skull.

Next to these beautiful flowers of betrayal.

There has been enough fucked up shit for one day. There is only so much I can take. Seeing this skull—knowing Draco gets pleasure in shit like this—it proves that I don't belong here.

I don't belong to him—a man that is proud of killing loved ones.

I don't know what the fuck Daddy saw in him, but I just don't see it. And I don't fucking get it. I'm starting to think Daddy was a fucking fool. Anyone can clearly see that Draco can't be trusted.

For all I fucking know, he killed Daddy and is trying to pretend he was close to him. He and his mother could be lying just to keep me on a leash, but what would be the point of that?

I don't say another word. I turn with haste and storm away, and I don't stop until I make it up to my bedroom, have curled up beneath the blanket, and have cried myself to sleep.

I don't care that I miss dinner.

I don't care that my stomach growls with hunger.

I just don't fucking care anymore. I can't take this. I can't do it—constantly betraying a husband that was nothing but good to me, in order to survive.

I miss him so fucking much.

Why did he have to be involved in this crappy drug and mafia business? Why couldn't he just be normal?

Oh, that's right.

S. WILLIAMS

Because normal men don't excite me.

Normal is boring.

Normal has never been a part of my life.

Normal, just like love, is fucking *useless*.

DAY THIRTEEN

I'm dreading this morning.

Yesterday was a horror fest and I don't think I can stomach much more, but I have no choice right now.

There was another note in my room when I woke up, no flowers this time. The curtains weren't drawn open either.

You had your time alone last night.

Be at breakfast on time and dressed properly.

-Draco

That's what the note said, but I ripped it up and tossed it in the trashcan.

After I'm all cleaned up, I get dressed and then brush my hair until the waves are loose.

I look towards the chocolate cosmos again.

I hate those flowers now. I want them gone.

I pick them up and then rush to the bathroom, dumping them in the trashcan where the note is.

The water trickles into the bin as well. I watch it all disappear and satisfaction courses through me.

I swing around and walk to the door. Gripping the doorknob, I swing the door open and walk down the hallway. I have more than enough time to make it to breakfast. I know if I miss breakfast too, Draco won't be so kind.

I took it as a sign that I could have my moment last night because he didn't bother me anymore after what happened in the garden of cosmos. I didn't even hear him walk past my bedroom at 2 a.m. He left me completely alone and I was glad.

As I trot down the stairs, pretending I'm okay, I make a sharp right and slam right into someone's back.

The person's bulky body turns around slowly, his familiar stacked shoulders causing me to take a leap back. His dark, coal-black eyes bolt on me and he glares. He glares so hard I feel like he's watching my soul cry out for help.

His bald head is shiny with minor scars. There are faint yellow and purplish bruises around his eyes. There is a bandage across the bridge of his nose, and his upper lip is slightly swollen.

Behind him is Bain, and he watches me with a narrowed gaze, looking me up and down in my maxi skirt and cami.

My eyes flicker over to the first man again.

It's Axe Man.

A chill cloaks my entire body.

He says absolutely nothing to me as I walk past him and Bain.

Bain I can feel watching me, his disgusting gaze making my stomach form into knots. When I get closer to the dining room, I take one glance back and they are both still staring my way.

Axe Man grimaces.

Bain smirks.

I snatch my line of sight away and hurry into the dining room.

Seeing Draco sitting at the head of the table somewhat relieves me, but trust me, I am still pissed at him. He watches me come closer and when his eyes dip around me to look at them, he narrows his gaze.

I hope the frustration is on my face. I hope he can tell that I'm not comfortable with them around, especially Axe Man. He looked at me as if he wanted to eat me alive.

I sit down and scratch at my cuticles. Francesca isn't here but I wonder what's keeping her. She normally beats me to the table.

"What's wrong?" Draco asks calmly.

I look up. "Nothing. I'm fine," I lie.

"Did they say something to you?" He gestures towards where Bain and Axe Man were standing. They aren't there anymore.

"Nothing at all."

Draco scans me thoroughly. He doesn't believe me. But this time it's true. They didn't say anything…but their looks shouted it all.

"Just wondering where Francesca is," I add in. What a load of bullshit.

"Not feeling well," he informs me. "She gets intense migraines."

"Oh."

He sits up in his chair. "She suffered a few concussions before she came here under my roof. Ever since, she's been getting migraines more often."

"Are they bad?"

"I had to buy black out curtains for the room she's in, so yes. Very bad."

"Oh." My lips twist. At least he's sympathetic. "You still…let her eat, don't you?"

His laughter bellows, filing the empty spaces of the dining room. "Gianna, I know you think I'm a monster, but I wouldn't deny her food because of something she can't control." He rubs his thumb and forefinger together, glancing at his mother. "Someone I knew well used to deal with migraines. I used to be a witness to the pain they caused. I don't take them lightly."

I bob my head, pleased to hear that.

When I see how he looks at his mother and how she smiles faintly at him, I realize he's probably talking about his father.

The butlers come out with the food and we dig in without many words to rub together. I can feel Draco glancing at me every so often as he eats and drinks. I'm certain he's thinking about yesterday.

He should know that I will never forgive him.

I am just a prisoner here, and he hates that he wants me so much.

"I want to go to the city today," Mrs. Molina says in Spanish, lowering her fork. "There's a new flea market. I could use more thread and needles. I would like to make some more quilts."

"Yes, mama. You can go. Just make sure you take Patanza and Diego with you."

She frowns. "I don't like being around Patanza. She is disrespectful and always rushes me." She chews her eggs before speaking again. "I still think you should fire her."

He sighs. "You know I can't, mama."

"Why not?"

"Because she has nowhere to go."

"So what? She is an angry, uncontrollable woman with a dirty mouth—"

"She works for me. I can control her very well. She won't be fired and that's the last time I will tell you this." His eyebrows draw together as he picks up his apple juice. "She won't go with you to the flea market. I will tell Guillermo to go in her place."

Mrs. Molina presses her lips and continues eating, as if she's satisfied with that idea.

"Why doesn't Patanza have anywhere to go?" I ask in English.

Both of them look up at me when I ask my question.

Mrs. Molina's eyes are wide with astonishment and Draco's lips smash together as he grips his fork and knife. He starts to cut into his pancakes, keeping a careful eye on me.

"Why does it matter to you?" he asks after a few chomps.

"Just curious."

He swallows what's left and then gulps down the remainder of his juice. "I knew her in school. Since I was twelve. She was never accepted by her family. Her mother abandoned the family when she was born and her father...did things to her that he shouldn't have. When she sees the role of a mother being portrayed, she gets very defensive and uncomfortable. Which is why mamá doesn't like her. I agreed to take her in, make sure she's fed, clothed, washed, just as long as she does what I need her to do around here. In return, she gives me her respect, her loyalty, and her life if need be."

"Oh. Sorry to hear that," I whisper.

"Don't be. It's made her stronger. A woman with a heart and soul of steel." Draco seems proud of that quality.

"Does she love you like Francesca does?" I know I've just pushed the line with my question, so I'm not surprised when the amusement drips off his face and his glare becomes solid and heavy.

"I haven't *fucked* her, Gianna, if that's what you're implying."

"Draco," Mrs. Molina lightly scolds.

I shrug as if I don't care, but really it does matter to me, especially when he keeps jamming his cock inside my body and mouth. I don't know what those girls have. For all I know they are carrying unknown STDs or diseases.

"El amor es la muerte," he grumbles, watching me intently. "You know what that means?"

I don't respond. I'm too focused on his grim features.

"Love is death. Loving anyone or anything too much will get you or the person you love, killed. Love, Gianna, is useless. Like I said before."

"That's not true," I declare.

"Oh, it's very true and you know it. First your mother, and then Lion, and now…Toni." My heart shrivels up in my chest and I cringe inside, holding his gaze. "Who will be next before you realize love is nothing more than one big fucking illusion?"

My eyes prick with hot tears. When will he stop being a fucking jackass already? It's over with. It's done, yet he keeps shoving their deaths in my face. If he had so much respect for Daddy, why is he being this way towards me?

Acting like a fucking bully.

I shove out of my chair and stand up straight. "May I be excused?"

He flicks his fingers, encouraging me to disappear. And then he stands and says something to Mrs. Molina in Spanish. She nods her head in return, and they both treat me as if I'm a ghost now.

I stare at him, though. I stare for so long. I don't know why. I just can't believe he's this way. He lost his father young. Okay, big deal. So did I. That doesn't justify why he is the way he is. There has to be more—more than he and even Mrs. Molina are willing to confess.

I look between the two of them—the confusing bond they have—and then I finally take off, not once looking back.

I clomp up the stairs and as soon as I step around the corner, I press my back against the wall and drag in a few breaths. I need to find a way out of here.

I take a look around. No windows, but there is a set of double doors beyond where my bedroom is.

It's at the end of the hallway, about thirty steps from where I am. The doors have short, square windows on them. There are bright rays of sunlight spilling through the slits between the curtains.

I scamper down the hallway and grip the gold knobs, bursting right in. The room is vacant, so I step ahead, taking a look around for bodies.

The curtains are gold, the furniture black. There is a desk in the corner with paper on top of it that catches my attention. An ink pen is on the paper, but there are no words on it.

I smile just a little, stepping closer.

Writing was my form of escape.

Poems. Short stories. As long as romance is included, I enjoy it immensely.

I walk towards the desk, but then I hear something unordinary.

Gasping.

Panting.

Groaning.

Sighing.

I turn towards the sound and that's when I smell something thick in the air. My eyes immediately dart over to the door on the east wall. It's shut. I walk towards it slowly, eyebrows thinning.

I shouldn't be nosey. I shouldn't care…but I have to know.

My fingers wrap around the doorknob and I snatch it open. There is another room inside. It's not as big as the one I was just in, but it's still a decent size. It's darker in this room, mainly because none of the lights are on.

There is a brown leather sofa perched against the wall.

PASSION & VENOM

And there are people on top of it.

Brown curls with honey streaks flop from side to side, her ass cheeks slamming down, jiggling with the momentum.

She's trying to be quiet on purpose—she, as in *Francesca*.

She gasps sharply as she looks back and spots the open door.

I stand with my chin practically sitting to the ground now, and when she scrambles off his lap, that's when I see *him*.

Bain's sweaty white hair clings to his forehead. He pushes her away completely and then climbs to a stand, stomping in my direction.

I dash away from the room and through the double doors before he can catch me. Fortunately he's slow because his pants are bunched around his ankles. He's not quick enough.

I rush back down the stairs, hurrying towards the dining area. But when I get there, Draco isn't there anymore and neither is Mrs. Molina.

Now, I'm no snitch, but this is my chance to get Bain the fuck out of here. Francesca has been a bitch to me lately so as of now I don't give a shit what happens to her.

If me giving him their dirty little secret is enough to make him stop being a jackass, maybe even gain me some freedom, and also make him forget about the wreck from yesterday, then so be it.

I'm turning into one snitch-ass-bitch.

"You stupid fucking bitch!" A hand squeezes my arm and yanks me around. Bain hauls me down the hallway, but I claw at him, screaming.

He cups my mouth, gripping my arm tighter. "Stop fucking fighting and shut the fuck up!"

I bite his fingers and he roars, slinging me away. I land on the hard marble floor, my back hitting the edge of the wall, but he storms for me again, dragging me towards the den by the ends of my hair.

My feet kick and scramble to get away. He has my hair locked in his hands, tugging it tight. My roots feel like they are about to be ripped out.

Jesus!

Where is Draco when I fucking need him!

I won't get hurt, that's what he promised me. He fucking lied.

Bain shoves me down on the sofa and then leans forward, pointing a stern finger at me. Francesca appears behind him with her arms folded. She only has on a black robe.

Her eyes are frantic though. They are a dead giveaway. She's afraid. She knows that I know now. We are no longer on the same fucking team. We are officially enemies.

Traitorous bitch.

"You even think about telling him, and I will gut you like a fucking fish, bitch. I will pack you in that goddamn van and take you to town, fuck the shit out of you, beat the shit out of you, fuck you again, and then sell you for everyone else to do what the hell they want to do to you. I will fucking *end* you, do you got that?"

I grimace up at him. "Fuck you!" I spit. "Draco!" I scream, hoping he'll hear me and answer. Praying to God that he's still around somewhere. He can't be too far.

Bain stands up straight, shaking his head. "Draco is already in his car and driving away, dumb cunt. That was your only fucking warning. Get up." He grips my arm and jerks me up.

I fight against him, but he only holds on tighter, even as I swing for his face.

He walks down a hallway in the den, away from the light. It gets much darker as we keep going.

"Let me go!" I try and wriggle out of his grasp again as he forces me down the rickety staircase, but it's impossible. He's holding me so tight there will surely be bruises forming.

When he knocks on a door, it immediately swings open, someone large appears, and my heart fucking fails me.

Axe Man turns around, standing there, eyes on me.

He wears a look—one that clearly shouts he is going to ruin my fucking life just as I did his.

His jaw is pulsing now, nostrils red at the edges. He is ready to tear me to shreds.

"Stop!" I scream, digging my heels into the ground. "Leave me alone!"

Bain shoves me forward and I land on my knees and palms. I pull myself up rapidly, dashing to the corner.

This room is dark with a foul odor. The walls are a dark shade of gray. It's cold in here.

It's some sort of cellar, but there is absolutely nothing inside of it. Nothing but a single folding chair.

"He's gone?" Axe Man asks, his voice gruff.

"Gone all day. Won't be back for another six hours. Have your fucking way and don't be fucking easy on her." Bain sneers.

They both look at me with lust-pervaded eyes. Francesca appears moments later, touching Bain's shoulder.

"Bain...maybe you should wait until he has another big trip. Draco will find out. She'll tell him."

"Not if we kill her first."

I pant unevenly, my eyes stretching wider.

"We'll say she got away," he continues in Spanish. "We'll cut the tracker out, put it somewhere for him to find later with a little bit of her blood on it. He'll believe she cut it out and ran after the shit she pulled yesterday with Morales' car."

Francesca swallows hard as I back away to the corner, as if her mouth is suddenly full of cotton. Axe Man walks towards me, closing me in.

He has a sneer on his lips, one that makes me want to vomit all that I ate not too long ago. Francesca finally backs away and when I hear her steps drifting up the staircase, I want to slice her fucking throat open.

I knew that bitch couldn't be trusted. I thought she had a good heart. Does she even love Draco? Or is she so hypnotized and owned by him that she feels nothing at all for anyone else?

Anyone that can love shouldn't let this happen!

Then again...this is exactly what she needs to happen.

She needs me gone so she can have him all to herself again. Now that I think about it, maybe this same thing happened to the other girl. Maybe she never ran away. Maybe they teamed up and killed her so Francesca could be the only one again.

"I'll keep watch," Bain announces. "Make sure you hurry the fuck up—and save some of that pussy for me. I've been dying to get inside it."

Axe Man's eyes spark. "With a pretty bitch like this it shouldn't take me long to bust a big fucking nut inside her."

Bain grins sinisterly in my direction and then he walks out, shutting the heavy door behind him.

There is a dim light in the far corner, but other than that it becomes even darker. Axe Man stands above me, and in an instant he yanks me up and shoves me against the wall.

My legs quake uncontrollably. I search for something to use against him, but he has no weapons on him.

That is probably the price he has to pay from Draco. No weapons until he redeems himself. Well, he's doing a terrible fucking job at trying to get within Draco's good graces.

"I will get out of here alive," I seethe, "and I will make sure Draco knows all about what you did to me. He'll be pissed to know you put your cock anywhere near me."

Axe man chuckles and then grips the front of my cami. He rips the fabric apart with his large, ugly hands, as if it's a sheet of paper. The sound of it seems to echo off the walls and my stomach caves in on itself.

"You think I give a fuck?" He steps back, observing my breasts. Then he reaches forward, unclasping it from the front.

When my breasts are freed, I look away, still searching for something. Anything. There is only the chair.

I could use that chair, smash his head in with hit, but I have to be quick.

Axe Man shoves me against the wall as that thought runs through my mind and the back of my head hits it, dazing me.

When my body sags from the blow, he yanks my skirt down and my bare legs are instantly chilled by the exposure.

"I've been waiting for this for a long fucking time, *puta*." *Bitch*.

His grin is revolting. He grabs my arm and then twists me around to bend me over. I feel his hardness rubbing across my lower back.

I let him do this, but my eyes don't move from that chair.

My vision blocks out all else but the folded seat.

My heart is thundering, and his cock pushes into my ass some more. My fingernails scrape the wall, my breaths thick as he grips the waistband of my panties and yanks viciously.

"Be smart, baby girl. Never foolish. Think fast. Don't hesitate. First instinct is always right in our world. If you are ever in any danger, you think about what Daddy would do."

Daddy...

Those words.

I was eleven when he said that to me, and I will never forget it. I got into my first fistfight at the age of fourteen. I beat her up so bad that I was expelled from school and forced to transfer to another. The other schools didn't want me, so Mom home schooled me.

It was the best decision she ever could have made.

She said it every single day we had class in the kitchen over hot meals and snacks.

Think about what Daddy would do.

I've seen Daddy in action.

I've seen him angry.

I've also seen Toni angry and neither of them held back on their actions.

They unleashed a wrath like none other.

They destroyed without thought—demolished without restraint.

It used to confuse me to know they killed. I used to hate Daddy for coming home with bloodstains on his shirt and a gun with a hot barrel.

I used to be furious when Toni would say it was just business and that it had to be done.

But now...I get it.

Because twisted, sick fucks like Axe Man don't deserve second chances.

Twisted fucks like him deserve to *die*.

When I hear his belt buckle jingle, that's when I make my move.

His hand is on the base of my skull, forcing my cheek on the cold wall as he tugs at his zipper and squirms out of his pants and underwear.

But he's a fool to think I'm weak. I got him before. What makes him think I can't again, but much worse this time?

When he pulls that hand away, I elbow him in the face, dip from in front of him, and dash for the chair.

He grunts and chases after me, catching me by the hair and yanking me back. When he gathers me in his arms, he punches me square in the face with a large fist, returning the vicious blow.

Blood leaks down my already fucked-up nose.

My mouth instantly aches, and I cry out, shoving against him.

I don't stop fighting. Because Daddy wouldn't stop fighting. Toni wouldn't stop. Momma didn't give up or give in to her disease, even when she knew she was going to die.

"GET OFF OF ME!" I scream, clawing at his face, using all of my strength.

"Shut the fuck up!" He grunts heavily as he marches forward and shoves my face on the wall again. He presses my naked body on it and then something hard presses into the center of my asshole.

The dry run he shoves in is so fucking painful that a heavy gasp fills the cellar.

He has his disgusting cock in my ass, my hair in his hands, and he slams in roughly, stretching me wider.

"You are the most hardheaded bitch I know. Just shut the fuck up and *take it*!" he barks as I shriek in pain. "You can stab me, fight me, and even have Draco beat the fuck out of me, but you knew by the end of this shit I would get what the fuck I wanted."

He buries his face into my hair and inhales my scent.

But I can't even be repulsed by it because the unwanted tears streaming down my face are hot and thick and they tell me everything. I am afraid. I can't do anything.

His cock is shoving in deeper and deeper. He has me pressed so close that I can barely breathe.

Even as I squirm, I can't find a way out.

I keep looking towards the chair, hoping—no, *begging* it to come closer. But it's still there. Too far to reach.

He grunts harder, plunges further, his rough skin clapping on my backside.

"Fuck, you have a tight ass. I knew it would be. Tight as fuck. Now it's time to feel that tight fucking cunt of yours too."

He yanks himself out, gripping the back of my neck with one hand, using the other to spread my legs further apart. He's breathing heavily, trying to aim for my most sacred area, but I won't let him have it.

I jerk my hips sideways—anywhere away from him.

He becomes angry and draws my upper body back just to slam my face into the hard wall again. I feel my stitches pop, and my nose cracks again. Blood drips down from somewhere—I don't know where.

He presses his cock at my entrance, but I jerk sideways again.

"Stop!" I croak, but it's useless and barely audible.

He slams my face on the wall again, trying to get to me to cooperate. I don't give up though.

He pushes one of his knees down on the back of my thigh and glides his cock into my ass again.

Rougher, drier strokes.

I whimper, and then cry out again, my hair blending with the tears.

His sweat drips down my back as he leans in and sucks the skin on my shoulder. He's pumping in and out of me, and I wail for somebody—*anybody*—to help.

I don't know what to do.

I don't even know if I should fight it any longer.

Draco isn't even here.

How can he save me when he's not fucking here?!

I'd much rather have him take me. If he comes and makes this stop, I will willingly hand myself over to him. I won't deny him any longer. I won't refuse him. I won't even put up a guard against him.

I will do what he wants, which is accept this fate.

Accept this life.

Accept...*him.*

I swear it.

Axe Man has me pinned, moving in and out. My body slams violently against the wall, crashing against it. I wish I could melt into it. I wish I could disappear.

He dips down a bit to slide his cock between my legs. I have my thighs crushed together so tightly that he can't get through completely. I won't let him get there. Fuck that.

A banging noise comes from the left, a loud and heavy thud.

It sounds like someone is stomping down the stairs.

It's probably Bain, coming for his fix. I wouldn't be surprised, but the thought terrifies me. I won't be able to hold off both of them.

The door flies open.

A tall figure stands between the frames and hot brown eyes look in our direction.

Something hot and wet spills down my back and I realize it's Axe Man's come.

He releases me in an instant, backing away as Draco charges forward. I sink down to my knees, watching as Draco meets up to Axe Man with a machete in his right hand.

He shouts something in Spanish. I'm too out of it to comprehend at first, but he is furious and there are angry words—words that he would probably never say around his mother.

"Jefe, no—por favor—" Please? He's begging? That stupid fucking pig.

"Gianna," Draco calls, stepping towards me. But I'm so lifeless—so feeble. I can't respond. My mouth feels dry. My throat has closed in on itself.

My brain is in denial about what just happened.

This didn't happen, did it?

It couldn't have. How could he let this happen?

Draco's eyes burn as he looks down at me. I stare up at him, desperate.

Helpless.

Damaged.

And done.

Just...*done*.

And the sad fact is, he knows it.

His fingers tighten around the handle of the machete, his nostrils reddening at the edges. He turns rapidly as Axe Man scrambles on his palms and knees towards the open door.

Draco lifts the machete above his head and then he brings it down.

Shwack.

A clean slice, right through the neck.

Blood gushes, and Axe Man's bald, scarred head hits the ground with a heavy *thunk*, rolling right beside my leg.

"Pinche hijo de puta!" *Fucking son of a bitch*. Draco is livid, still slicing parts of Axe Man, butchering him limb by limb.

I feel blood splattering on me. Everywhere. I should stop him…but I won't. I refuse. This has to be done.

He doesn't stop until there is nothing left but bits and pieces of him.

There is blood pooled on the floor. Body parts surround me—fingers and arms.

When I look up, Draco is in such a rage that I think he's going explode. Blood is all over his white button-down shirt, splattered on his face and drenching the sharp edge of the machete, his chest rising and sinking rapidly.

His eyes dart over to me again as I hold still in the corner. The blood surrounds me, but he snatches me right up and into his arms.

"Fuck, Gianna. I never should have walked out of that fucking door." My head bobs up and down, my ass burning as he takes me up the stairs.

He storms through the den and makes his way up the next staircase to get to the bedrooms.

But instead of going to my room, he maneuvers left, takes a few more steps down the hall, and then enters another.

The door opens soundlessly. He slams and locks it behind him but doesn't stop walking.

I can't think right now.

I've been violated. I've been put in a position I've never been in before.

Daddy never would have let this happen, and neither would Toni.

I don't feel like myself.

I don't even know who I am anymore.

I tried to fight.

Yes, Gia, you tried to fight.

But it wasn't enough.

No, it wasn't enough.

That's not what Lion would do, Gia, baby. Toni's voice echoes in my head, ringing loudly.

Fuck you! You are supposed to be here. You are supposed to be protecting me.

You...are the reason this happened, Toni! This is all your fault!

I must be out of my mind.

Maybe it was all a nightmare.

Maybe I'm not fully awake and I'm still in my bedroom, trying to forget about what was done to Kevin by replacing it with something much worse.

"Gianna?" A deep voice filters through my subconscious. Draco's voice.

He sits me down on top of the bathroom counter. I don't look up at him, but I do wince when I feel the pain again.

I hear him curse in Spanish and then he walks away. Water starts moments later. It runs for a while. I can feel the steam building up.

I stare down at the floor, listening to my rapid heartbeat. Feeling my dignity withering away.

He stole from me. Axe Man. He stole my confidence. My pride. He did something to me that I wanted to save for someone I trusted. My husband.

He...may have just ruined me.

The stronger, better parts of me.

The parts of me still willing to fight just to get out of this hell.

Gianna... Gianna... "Gianna!"

I whip my head up and look into Draco's eyes.

Sorrow is there, a small trace. He looks me up and down, and when I look up I realize I'm now in an oval bathtub. It's wide enough to fit three people.

The water is milky and hot enough to sear away the grime and blood...but not hot enough to make me forget.

"You...left, Draco," I choke out.

His worry fades, and in an instant he snatches himself away, pacing the bathroom. This bathroom is much bigger. It's nicer.

"I didn't go far. I said I would be gone for most of the day but I only did it to see what Pico would do while I was away. I knew I couldn't trust him. I was just hoping I wouldn't have to kill two people in less than twenty-four hours."

I stare down at my toes at the end of the tub. "You said I would be protected. That nothing would happen while I'm here, under your protection."

"I know what the fuck I said."

So why weren't you here!?" I snap, and I don't realize how loud I am until I hear my voice echoing off the walls. I stand up rapidly and the water drips down my bare body. "He *raped* me, Draco! He took from me, to hurt you! And Bain! God, Bain! He was in on it. And so was Francesca! But you leave him here as your eyes and ears while you're away?"

He looks shocked to hear this, as if he didn't know Bain and Francesca were a part of this. I shake my head from side to side. How can he be so fucking stupid? They were doing shit right up under his nose and he didn't even notice.

"The very people that you claim loyal and respectful are your biggest fucking enemies. You have them roaming this house—Bain calls me names and threatens how he wants to fuck and then sell me! Francesca hates me because she loves you and I'm stealing the attention away! She wants to see me dead!"

I step out of the tub, storming towards him.

I've had enough of this life.

I've had enough of trying to please him and belittling myself just to make him feel better.

After what just happened, I'd much rather be fucking dead than bowing down to him.

"Why the fuck didn't you tell me about Bain before?!" His voice is angry.

"I didn't think there was anything to tell. You are their boss and they all think I'm just your play toy. You punish me, fuck me over, bully, and torture me. You claim you will protect me, but that's bullshit. If you treat me like shit, why wouldn't they do the same?"

He's breathing raggedly through flared nostrils. I'm panting way too quickly, fire brewing in my veins.

"You knew my father," I go on. "You knew him well, and that is probably the only reason I am still standing here. But if he was here right now, he would fucking murder you with his bare hands for what has been done to me. He would rip your fucking tongue out and feed it to his hounds. He would make sure that you are *nothing* and will never amount to anything again. He. Would. Fucking. *Destroy*. You."

Draco's eyes fill with ferocity. He takes the last step forward, and as his head cocks, he says, "But he isn't here anymore...is he?"

My hearts drops.

"He can't do any of that shit. So ask yourself who's in charge now? Who is the only person you can rely on?" He cups the back of my neck, angling my head up so I can look at him. "It's not Toni. It's not Lion. It's me, Gianna. Me. You know it. Lion knew it. Everyone knows it. I made a mistake by thinking I could leave you here without extra protection and I am admitting my faults. But don't think I will take this lightly. Don't think I will be gentle about this."

"You're right. You did make a mistake!" I shove him on the chest, furious now. "You say that you want to make me yours—that you want me to yourself. You tell them I'm off limits, but you don't have the heart to prove it! You want me to be yours, then *make me yours*! That means you shouldn't let anyone touch me! Don't let anyone near me! You should be making me so sacred to them that they worship the fucking ground I walk on!"

He doesn't speak, and his grip slacks on the back of my neck. This is the first time I've seen Draco speechless. Utterly speechless.

"What I saw—what he did to you—it was unacceptable and he has paid for it...and so will they," he says, and it sounds like cheap words to me.

"How?" I demand. "Tell me how!"

He drops his chin, his hot gaze holding mine. "You are the woman I want and I am probably the most wanted man in the fucking world. I am being chased, watched, and hunted by people I don't even know. And you know what? I don't give a single fuck. Because that makes people *afraid* of me. So afraid that even you, Gianna, should be afraid of what I am going to do to them. Pico was only the beginning. He got out of it way too easily, and that is only because I was too furious to hold back."

"What will you do to them?" I demand again, jutting my chin out.

"You'll find out soon. But you have to promise me one thing."

"What?"

"Accept your fate. You are not weak. You are strong, and I can tell by the way you stand here, facing me after what just happened, that you are a lot stronger than you'd like to believe. You are a powerful, bold, and relentless woman, and you are right. You *are* mine." He cups my ass in his hands. I don't wince, even though I feel raw and exposed there. I let him do this, and I burn inside with some sort of passion I haven't felt in ages.

"Accept me, and I will accept you," he murmurs. "Devote yourself to me, and I will be sure that this never fucking happens again. I will make that vow to you. I will swear it on my father's grave and my mother's soul. As long as you say you are mine, I will do whatever your heart desires."

"Did you let him do that to me just so I could accept this fate?" I am still angry, and untrusting, shoving his hand away.

He's pissed.

He pushes me against the wall and his forehead presses down hard on mine. "I cut him to fucking pieces and I will do it again in a heartbeat to *anyone* that tries to fuck the woman I want."

I swallow hard, the pit of my belly fluttering.

He lowers his gaze to my lips, grabbing my shoulders. "It was too quiet when I walked through that door, Gianna. I didn't see him or you. There was only one place he'd hide. He was lingering around the den. He had this planned—*they* had this planned. But what they've failed to realize is that they have fucked with the wrong man. They all did…and they know it. And now they will fucking pay."

"I want them gone—I don't care how," my voice trembles.

He catches my quivering bottom lip. "And that will happen. You'll see."

I nod, dropping my gaze.

"Accept," he whispers against my lips. "Let me truly make you mine."

I pick my head up, locking eyes with him. Something swirls inside them. Something hot and desirable. I've never seen this look on him before. It's desperate—almost hopeful.

My teeth clamp into my bottom lip, but without any hesitation at all, I run my hands down his forearms and then entwine our fingers.

"I accept, Draco."

His sculpted lips incline at the corners. Instead of taking me victoriously like a savage would, he squeezes my hand and leads the way back to the tub.

"Get in." I step forward, looking up at him. I guide my body into the warm water. It's not as hot as before.

He walks towards a small cabinet and takes down a body sponge. When he comes back, he squats down beside the tub and then reaches across me to pick up the bar of soap.

After lathering the soap on the sponge, he reaches forward and starts to wash me. I watch the suds surround me and then look up.

His face is concentrated. Stern. I can't read his expression. He runs the sponge from my neck to my breasts, scrubbing me gently around them, and then under my arms. He continues down to my sacred area, but then he pauses, eyes flashing up to me.

"Did he touch you right here?" He asks this in Spanish.

I shake my head. "He tried," I respond. "I fought."

He swallows thickly, and then continues down, running over the mound. His hand disappears into the water, but I feel him there, his fingers. The sponge.

His eyes flicker up to mine as he washes me around the sensitive area.

"Lift up," he commands, and I rest my elbows on the edge of the tub to lift my hips. He runs the sponge over my plump cheeks and when he lowers down to the crease and runs it through my raw bottom, I wince. "It's okay, niñita. Let me take care of you."

I barely nod, watching him intently. Our eyes hold for the longest time, and something swims inside of his. He's angry, yes, but there is remorse there. The guilt—it's eating him alive.

Despite my bad behavior and foul mouth, he hates what has been done to me.

When he finishes up, he drops the sponge and then leans forward. His mouth is less than an inch away from mine, and he studies me carefully.

"I will make sure they beg for your forgiveness and then die a vengeful death for their disobedience and lack of respect."

I bob my head.

"I mean it, Gianna. I won't be easy on them. I will make them fucking suffer."

"I know," I whisper. And really, I do know. I've witnessed his wrath firsthand.

He sighs and draws back, standing to his feet. He walks to a cabinet and grabs a small black box. Opening he, he digs through it and take something small out. "I think it's time to explain some things to you," he murmurs as he places it back on the shelf inside the cabinet.

"Things like what?"

He comes back in my direction and when he lowers his hand, he places the object down on the edge of the tub. I look down at it, and when I see the familiar diamond ring, my chest squeezes tight. "About your ex-husband...and your father," he says.

I freeze for a split second, pulling my line of sight away from it. "What about them?"

"You'll find out as soon as I take care of this. I need to send someone to clean that mess in the cellar. I will be back, though. Just make sure you stay in this room—*my* room. Don't go anywhere else."

He steps forward and tips my chin, stroking my hair back. Sincerity runs deep in his brown irises. He feels awful, I think. That's what it seems. His devotion is too fierce.

He feels bad that Pico took from me, something that I will never get back. He's probably fueled with jealousy and spite.

"I have no doubt that you fought." His voice is low and even. "You are your father's daughter and one thing he told me and my family is that, boy or girl, he would never raise a coward."

A coward, I am not.

He pulls away and stands up straight.

I want to thank him, but for what? I was still taken.

I felt so weak down in that cellar. So vulnerable and...*used*.

I already want to forget it, but it's too fresh in my mind. His hot breath, his greasy sweat, his disgusting mouth on my skin. I squeeze my eyes shut, lowering my head.

"I will be back as soon as possible, niñita. Wait for me." He pulls his hand away and plants a kiss on the top of my head, exhaling deeply. He walks towards the door, glancing back once. "Don't leave this room," he commands lightly. "I mean it."

"I won't."

He nods once, and with slight reluctance, he finally walks out of the bathroom while stripping out of his bloodstained shirt. When he's gone, I fear the loneliness.

The quiet. I hope he really does come right back. I need his protection.

I look at the ring again, blinking slowly. I stare at it for a while. He's giving it back, but the question is do I want it?

The past. The memories. The heartache.

I flick the ring and it clinks loudly on the tile floor. I then sink down lower in the tub, staring at the water. My knobby knees are quaking. My hands are trembling.

I accepted my fate.

There is no turning back now.

I sink down further, until the water has enveloped me whole. I stay this way for nearly one whole minute, not breathing. Not thinking. Not moving.

Eyes shut.

Airtight.

Heart booming.

And then I rise.

I gasp.

Water falls past my lips. I taste blood.

And I know…I know what I have to do.

I must become the woman to match Draco's exterior.

The one thing I've learned is that weak people don't last. And maybe he was right. Love is useless. Compassion is pointless. Mercy is redundant.

I've been kind.

I've understood.

I've been helpful.

I've been trying to stay positive, even through the worst of times.

But no more. I have accepted my fate. And that fate is to become just as dangerous and ruthless as Draco Molina.

My new partner.

My new *king*.

He can have all of me, just as long as I get to call the shots. Mind, body, and soul—it's all his. He can take it and cherish it because there is no looking back for me.

Toni…he is my past.

Daddy, he is in my heart. But Draco is right. He's gone too.

PASSION & VENOM

I am his heir.

I was passionate. Passion was what I knew. Passion and hope were what kept me going. But passion and hope have constantly fucked me over.

This princess is ready to snatch up the big crown and become the one thing she was deathly afraid of.

A queen. With veins full of venom and a heart full of ice.

A queen who will no longer bow down, but have everyone else kneeling at her feet.

The games are over.

I can't leave now.

The malevolence has only begun.

Gianna Ricci is no more.

But Gianna *Nicotera* is here, and she is hungry for a *massacre*.

The boss thinks he's safe, but he's far from it. I have accepted, but that doesn't make him a winner. *I will own that man.* I will make him do things for me he never thought he would do for a woman. And as soon as he's comfortable—as soon as I see he has fallen for me—I will *end* him. The most wanted man in the world will be dead.

I will be free.

And he will be nothing.

The fangs. The claws. The rage.

Passion or venom? And you ask me what my choice is?

The venom.

Every. *single. fucking. ounce* of it.

Printed in Great Britain
by Amazon